D0544021

TARANTULA

Now a major film by PEDRO ALMODÓVAR

THE SKIN I LIVE IN

Thierry Jonquet was born in Paris in 1954. An exponent of the French noir influenced by post-May 1968 politics, Jonquet became one of France's best-known crime writers. He died in 2009.

© Editions Gallimard

THIERRY JONQUET

TARANTULA

Translated from the French by
Donald Nicholson-Smith

A complete catalogue record for this book can
be obtained from the British Library on request

The right of Thierry Jonquet to be identified as the author
of this work has been asserted in accordance with
the Copyright, Designs and Patents Act 1988

Copyright © 1995 Editions Gallimard
Translation copyright © 2002 by Donald Nicholson-Smith

The characters and events in this book are fictitious. Any similarity to real
persons, dead or alive, is coincidental and not intended by the author.

All rights reserved. No part of this book may be reproduced, stored in a
retrieval system or transmitted in any form or by any means, electronic,
mechanical, photocopying, recording or otherwise, without the prior
permission of the publisher.

First published as *Mygale* in 1995 by Editions Gallimard, Paris

First published in this English translation as *Mygale*
in 2002 by City Lights Books, San Francisco

First published in the UK in this edition in 2011 by Serpent's Tail
First published in the UK as *Tarantula* in 2005 by Serpent's Tail,
an imprint of Profile Books Ltd
3A Exmouth House, Pine Street
London EC1R 0JH
www.serpentstail.com

ISBN 978 1 84668 794 5
eISBN 978 1 84765 763 3

Printed and bound in Great Britain by
CPI Bookmarque Ltd, Croydon, Surrey

MIX
Paper from
responsible sources
FSC
www.fsc.org
FSC® C020852

I

The Spider

1

Richard Lafargue paced slowly along the graveled walk. It led to a little pond set amidst the trees alongside the wall surrounding the property. It was a clear night, an evening in July, and a shining rain of milky stars frecked the sky.

Camouflaged by a group of water lilies, a pair of swans slept serenely, their necks folded beneath their wings, the slender female snuggled tenderly against the more imposing body of her mate.

Lafargue plucked a rose, briefly inhaled its sweetish, almost cloying perfume, then retraced his steps. Beyond the alley of lindens stood the house, a compact, squat, graceless mass. On the ground floor were the servants' quarters, where Lise, the maid, would be taking her meal. To the right, a pool of light and a muffled purr signaled the garage, where Roger, the chauffeur, had the engine of the Mercedes running. And then there was the main drawing room, whose dark curtains allowed but a few thin streaks of light to escape.

Lafargue looked up to the floor above and let his gaze linger on the windows of Eve's rooms. There was a delicate glow, and through a half-open shutter came a timid sound of music, the first bars of "The Man I Love"…

Lafargue repressed a gesture of irritation and, striding briskly, went into the house, slamming the front door behind him, almost running to the staircase, and holding his breath as he bounded up the stairs. Once on the second floor, he raised his fist, but then held back and resigned himself to knocking gently with the knuckle of a curled index finger.

He slid back the three bolts that, from the outside, barred the door to the set of rooms inhabited by the woman who was so determinedly turning a deaf ear to his calls.

Without making a sound, he closed the door and proceeded into the dressing room. It was plunged in obscurity, the only light a glimmer from a shade-covered desk lamp standing on the piano. At the far end of the adjoining bedroom, brutal neon from the bathroom threw a bright white slash on the farthest wall of the flat.

In the half-shadows, he made his way to the stereo and turned the volume down, interrupting the first notes of whatever tune followed "The Man I Love" on the record.

He controlled his anger, then murmured, in a neutral tone quite devoid of reproach, a nonetheless biting comment about the length of time reasonably needed to make up her face, pick out a dress, and select jewelry appropriate for the kind of evening affair to which he and Eve were invited.

He went on into the bathroom, stifling a curse when he saw the young woman luxuriating in a thick cocoon of bluish foam. He sighed. His eyes met Eve's for a moment; the defiance he thought he read there caused him to snigger. He shook his head in feigned amusement at her childishness and left the flat.

Back in the main drawing room on the ground floor, he fixed himself a scotch at a bar set up near the fireplace and downed it in one swallow. The spirit burned his stomach and tic-like movements worked in his face. Going over to the interphone connected to Eve's rooms, he pressed the button, then cleared his throat before pressing his mouth against the plastic mouthpiece and bellowing:

"For God's sake, hurry up, you piece of shit!"

Eve started violently as the two 300-watt speakers set into the dressing room walls blasted out Richard's yell.

She shivered, then unhurriedly got out of the vast circular bathtub and slipped into a black flannel robe. She went and sat at the dressing table and began to apply makeup, wielding the mascara brush with lively little gestures.

With Roger at the wheel, the Mercedes left the house in Le Vésinet and headed for Saint Germain. Richard observed Eve, indolent beside him. She was smoking nonchalantly, bringing her ivory cigarette holder to her elegant lips at regular intervals. The lights of the city penetrated the car's interior in intermittent flashes, streaking her black silk sheath dress with fugitive dashes of brilliance.

Eve held her head way back, and Richard glimpsed her face only when her cigarette glowed briefly red.

They did not intend to linger at a garden party put on by a cheap wheeler-dealer bent on signaling his existence to the landed gentry of the region. They meandered among the guests, with Eve on Richard's arm, to the accompaniment of soft music from a band set up on the grounds. People clustered around buffet tables arranged at intervals along the tree-lined walks.

There was no way of avoiding the odd social bloodsucker. They had no choice but to raise glasses of champagne in honor of the master of the house. Lafargue ran into several colleagues, including a member of the Medical Council. He allowed himself to be complimented on his most recent article in *The Practitioner.* He even agreed, during a lull in the conversation, to take part in a panel discussion on reconstructive breast surgery at the forthcoming round-table conference at Bichat. Later, he felt like kicking himself for accepting the invitation instead of politely refusing.

Eve kept her distance; she seemed to be in the clouds. But she relished the lustful glances that a few of the guests cast her way and took pleasure in responding with a barely perceptible pout of contempt.

She left Richard long enough to go over to the band and request "The Man I Love." By the time the song's soft and languid opening bars were struck up, she was back at Lafargue's side. A mocking smile came to her lips when pain registered on the doctor's face. He took her gently by the waist and drew her aside. But when the saxophonist began a plaintive solo it was all he could do not to slap his companion.

It was nearly midnight by the time they at last took leave of their host and returned to the house in Le Vésinet. Richard accompanied Eve as far as her bedroom. Sitting on the sofa, he watched her undress, at first mechanically, then more sensually—facing him, staring him down with an ironic smile.

Once naked, Eve planted herself directly in front of Richard, her legs apart and the thicket of her pubic hair level with his face. He shrugged, got up, and went to get a small pearly white box from its place on one of the book shelves. Eve stretched out on a mat laid on the floor. He came and sat cross-legged beside her, opening the box and withdrawing the long pipe, aluminum foil, and small waxy balls that it contained.

He delicately filled the pipe and held a flaring match beneath the bowl before passing it to Eve. She took long deep puffs. The sickly sweet odor filled the room. She turned on her side and curled up, staring at Richard.

Before long her gaze lost its sharpness as her eyes glazed over. Richard was already getting another pipe ready.

An hour later he left her, making sure to turn the knob twice on all three bolts. Back in his own bedroom, he undressed, too, then scrutinized his graying countenance in the mirror at some length. He smiled at his reflection, at his white hair and the many deep wrinkles that scored his features. He raised his open hands before him, and feigned ripping apart some imaginary object. In bed at last, he tossed and turned for hours before falling asleep at first light.

2

The maid, Lise, had the day off, so it was Roger who got breakfast ready that Sunday. He knocked for quite some time at Lafargue's door before getting a response.

Richard ate heartily, biting with relish into fresh croissants. He was in high spirits, an almost playful mood. He put on jeans and a light cotton shirt, slipped into loafers, and went out for a turn round the property.

The swans glided up and down the pond, coming to the edge when Lafargue appeared amid the lilacs. He tossed them some pieces of bread and crouched to feed them from his hand.

Then he went walking in the grounds. The solid beds of flowers were bright swathes of color across the freshly mown grass. Richard made his way toward the seventy-five-foot swimming pool that had been constructed at the far end of the garden. The street and even the neighboring houses were screened from view by the wall that completely enclosed the property.

He lit a Virginia cigarette and inhaled deeply. He indulged in a long mocking laugh before heading back to the house. In the servants' quarters Roger had set Eve's breakfast tray down on the table. In the drawing room, Richard pressed the button on the intercom and roared into it: "BREAKFAST! TIME TO GET UP!"

Then he went upstairs.

He unlocked the door and advanced into the bedroom, where Eve was still sleeping in the great four-poster bed. The sheets covered all but a small part of her face, and her thick curly brown hair was a dark patch on the mauve satin.

Lafargue sat down on the edge of the bed, placing the tray next to Eve. She moistened the tip of her lips with the orange juice and nibbled dolefully at a honey-spread zwieback.

"It's the twenty-seventh," said Richard. "The last Sunday of the month. Had you perhaps forgotten?"

Eve shook her head weakly, without looking at Richard. Her eyes were blank.

"All right. We leave here in three-quarters of an hour."

He left the flat. Back in the drawing room, he went across to the intercom.

"I said three-quarters of an hour! D'you hear me?"

Upstairs, Eve went rigid as she suffered through Richard's amplified tirade.

The Mercedes had been traveling for three hours when it left the highway and took a winding local road. The Norman countryside lay prostrate in the torpor of the summer sun. Richard opened a bottle of cold soda and offered some to Eve, who was dozing, her eyes half-closed. She declined, and he closed the door of the little refrigerator.

Roger drove fast but professionally. Before long, he pulled the car up outside a country mansion on the fringe of a small village. A patch of dense woodland surrounded the property, some of whose outbuildings, protected by iron railings, were not far at all from the hamlet's last houses. On the château's forecourt sat knots of people out enjoying the sunshine. Women in white blouses moved among them bearing trays laden with multicolored plastic glasses.

Richard and Eve ascended the broad flight of steps leading to the main entrance, went inside, and addressed themselves to a formidable lady receptionist at a hatch. She smiled at Lafargue, shook Eve's hand, and beckoned to a male nurse. The visitors followed the man into an elevator, which took them to the third floor. Before them stretched a long straight corridor punctuated by set-back doorways, each equipped with a rectangular observation panel of transparent plastic. Without a word, the nurse opened the seventh door on the left, then stepped back as the couple entered.

A woman sat on the bed—a very young woman, though her youth was belied by her wrinkles and hunched posture. She offered a pitiful image of premature aging. Deep crevices ravaged her otherwise still childlike face. Her hair was unkempt—thickly matted, with spikes here and there. Her bulging eyes rolled this way and that. Her skin was blotched with darkish crusty patches. Her lower lip trembled spasmodically, and her trunk rocked slowly back and forth with metronomic regularity. She wore only a blue cotton smock without pockets. Her bare feet slithered about in overlarge bedroom slippers adorned with pom-poms.

She seemed not to have noticed the entrance of her visitors. Richard sat down next to her and took her chin in his hand and turned her face toward him. The young woman was compliant, yet nothing in her expression or gestures betrayed the slightest feeling or emotion.

Richard put his arm around her shoulders and drew her to him. The rocking ceased. Eve, standing near the bed, was contemplating the countryside through the reinforced-glass window.

"Viviane," Richard murmured. "Viviane, my darling."

He rose suddenly, grasping Eve's arm and obliging her to look at Viviane, who had started her rocking again, wild-eyed.

"Give it to her," said Richard sotto voce.

Eve opened her handbag, produced a box of soft-centered chocolates and held it out to the woman, to Viviane.

Clumsily Viviane seized the box, tore off the top, and set about greedily eating one chocolate after another. She ate every one. Richard watched her in stupefaction.

"Come on," sighed Eve, "that's enough." And she pushed Richard gently out of the room. The male nurse was waiting in the corridor; he closed the door as Eve and Richard made their way back to the elevator. They returned to the reception window and exchanged a few pleasantries with the receptionist, then Eve signaled the chauffeur, who was leaning against the Mercedes, reading a sports paper. Richard and Eve took their places in the back, and the car set off along the local road to the highway, returned to the Paris area, and thence proceeded to the house in Le Vésinet.

Richard had locked Eve into her upstairs quarters and given the help the remainder of the day off. Now he was relaxing in the drawing room, picking at cold dishes Lise had prepared before she left. It was nearly five o'clock by the time he got into the driver's seat of the Mercedes and sped off toward Paris.

He parked near Place de la Concorde and went into a building on Rue Godot-de-Mauroy. Keys in hand, he climbed briskly to the fourth floor and let himself into a spacious studio apartment. The center of the room was taken up by a great circular bed with mauve satin covers, and the walls were adorned by a few erotic prints.

On the bedside table was a combined telephone and answering machine. Richard set the tape in motion and listened to the messages: throaty, breathless voices of men trying to reach Eve. He noted the times they proposed for appointments. Leaving the apartment, he went quickly down the stairs and returned to the car. Back at Le Vésinet, he went straight to the intercom and called Eve.

"Eve, listen! Three! For this evening!"

Richard went upstairs.

She was in her dressing room, intently painting a watercolor. A peaceful, pleasant landscape: a clearing flooded with light, with at the center of the picture, drawn in black pencil, the face of Viviane. Bellowing with laughter, Richard seized a bottle of red nail varnish from the dressing table and dashed the contents over the watercolor.

"You're never going to change, are you?" he murmured.

Eve had stood up and was now methodically putting away the brushes, paints, and easel. Richard pulled her to him, till her face almost touched his.

"I have to thank you from the bottom of my heart," he told her softly, "for the humility that allows you to yield to my desires as you do."

Eve's features froze; from her throat rose a long, hollow, plaintive moan. Then a gleam of anger flashed in her eyes.

"Leave me alone, you pimp bastard!"

"Ha! Very funny! No, really, I can't tell you how charming you are when you rebel."

She had detached herself from his embrace. She patted her hair back into place and straightened her clothes.

"All right, then. This evening? Is that what you really want? When do we leave?"

"Right away, of course."

❖

They said nothing to each other on the way. They were inside the studio apartment on Rue Godot-de-Mauroy before a word was uttered.

"Get yourself ready," ordered Lafargue. "They won't be long now."

Eve opened a closet and undressed. First putting her own clothes away, she proceeded to dress in long black thigh boots, black leather skirt, and fishnet stockings. She made herself up, using white face powder and bright red lipstick, then sat down on the bed.

Richard left the apartment and entered its twin next door, where a one-way mirror let him secretly observe whatever went on in the room where Eve was waiting.

Her first client, a wheezy storekeeper around sixty with a bright red face, arrived just over half an hour later. The second came only at nine-thirty—a provincial pharmacist who visited Eve regularly and wanted merely to see her strolling naked about in the room's confined space. The third—whom Eve was obliged to keep waiting after he had begged her over the phone to let him come over—was the scion of a good family, a repressed homosexual who became excited as he walked up and down using insulting language and masturbating. Eve's role was to walk beside him, holding his hand.

Behind his mirror, Richard exulted at the spectacle, laughing silently, pitching back and forth in a rocking-chair, and applauding whenever the young woman evinced a sign of disgust.

When it was all over, he rejoined her. She tossed her leather gear aside and donned a severely cut suit.

"That was perfect! You are always perfect! Marvelous—so patient! Come on, let's go."

Richard took Eve's arm and took her off to supper at a Slavic restaurant. He kept the Gypsy musicians clustered around their table well supplied with bills—the very same bills that Eve's clients had left earlier on the bedside table in settlement for services rendered.

Think back. It was a summer evening, horribly hot—and unbearably humid. A storm that wouldn't break. You took your motorcycle, intent on racing through the darkness. The night air, you thought, would feel good.

You went fast. The wind filled your shirt, whose tails flapped noisily. Insects smashed onto your glasses, onto your face, but at least you were no longer hot.

It took quite a while for you to become concerned about the two white headlights piercing the blackness in your wake. Two electric eyes focused on you, never leaving you for an instant. When you did feel anxiety, you gunned the engine of your 125 to the limit, but the car behind was powerful and had no difficulty keeping up.

As your initial anxiety turned to panic under the relentless scrutiny of those lights, you began zigzagging through the forest. You could see, in your rearview mirror, that the driver of the car was alone. He seemed to have no wish to close on you.

The storm finally arrived. Drizzle quickly gave way to driving rain. After every curve the car would reappear. Streaming with water, you were soon shivering. Your bike's gas gauge had started to flash ominously. You had fuel enough for a very few more kilometers. By this time you had changed course so many times that you were lost in the forest. You no longer had the slightest idea which way to go to get to the nearest village.

The road surface was slippery, and you slowed down. The car leaped toward you, overtaking you and almost forcing you to skid out onto the shoulder.

But you braked, and the bike spun around. As you started up again to leave the way you had come, you heard your pursuer's brakes squeal as he too turned and began trailing you once again. It was darkest night, and sheets of rain made it impossible to see the road ahead.

In desperation you tried to mount the embankment at the edge of the road, hoping you might escape through the trees, but you skidded in the mud, and the 125 fell on its side, and the engine cut out. You managed to right the machine, though it was not easy.

Back in the saddle, you kicked the starter pedal, but the fuel tank was empty. The beam of a powerful flashlight was roving across the underbrush. To your dismay, it fastened on you as you raced for the cover of a fallen tree. You fingered the blade in the shank of your boot—a Wehrmacht knife that you always carried...

Sure enough, the car had pulled up sharply on the road. You felt your stomach knot at the sight of a massive silhouette getting a gun into firing position. The barrel was pointing in your direction. The report melded with the thunder claps. The flashlight had been laid down on the car roof. It went out. You ran then and were soon out of breath. You ripped your hands as you tore your way through the brushwood. From time to time the flashlight would come on again behind you, illuminating your flight. You could no longer hear anything; your heart throbbed crazily; mud clung to your boots and slowed you down. The knife was clasped tightly in your fist.

How long did the chase go on? Gasping for breath, you leaped over fallen trees in the blackness. A trunk lying flat on the ground tripped you, and you went sprawling on the soaking earth.

Laid out in the mud, you heard that cry, which was more like a growl. He stamped on your wrist, crushing your hand under the heel of his boot. You released the knife, and he fell upon you, pushing your shoulders down with his hands. Then one hand moved to your mouth, the other was clamped about your throat, and a knee was driven into your flank. You tried to bite the palm of his hand, but your teeth closed on nothing but a clod of earth.

He continued to hold you tightly against him. The two of you remained like this, welded together, in the darkness...The rain stopped...

3

Alex Barny rested on a camp bed in an attic room. He had nothing to do, except wait. The chatter of the cicadas in the garrigue was an unrelenting racket. Through the window Alex could see the crooked silhouettes of olive trees in the night, forms fixed in bizarre poses. With his shirtsleeve, he mopped his brow, where pearls of acidic sweat had gathered.

A naked bulb dangling from a wire attracted clouds of mosquitoes; every fifteen minutes or so, Alex would get furious and bombard them with Fly-Tox. On the concrete floor, a large dark circle of squashed mosquitoes continued to grow, shot through with specks of red.

Alex struggled to his feet and, relying on a cane, hobbled out of his bedroom and down to the kitchen of the farmhouse, which was somewhere in the depths of the countryside between Cagnes and Grasse.

The fridge was well stocked with a variety of provisions. Alex took out a can of beer, pulled off the tab, and drank it down. Belching loudly, he opened another can and went outside. In the distance, beyond the olive-covered hillsides, the sea shone in the moonlight, sparkling beneath a cloudless sky.

Alex took a few cautious steps. His thigh subjected him to brief bouts of searing pain. The dressing dug into his flesh. For two days now there had been no pus, but the wound was reluctant to heal. The bullet had traversed the muscular mass, happily missing the femoral artery and the bone.

He leaned with one hand against the trunk of an olive-tree and urinated, spraying a column of ants engaged in the transport of an immense pile of twigs.

He began drinking once more, sucking on the can of beer, swilling the foam around his mouth, spitting it out. He sat down on a bench on the porch, puffing and blowing, belching once more. He fished a pack of Gauloises from his shorts pocket. The beer had splashed onto his T-shirt, already filthy with grease and dust. Through the cotton material, he pinched his stomach, taking a fold of flesh between thumb and forefinger. He was getting fat. Over the last three weeks of forced idleness, of nothing but sleeping and eating, he had been getting fat.

Alex ground his foot into a two-week-old newspaper on the floor. The heel of his hiking boots covered a face staring out from the front page: his own. Alongside the image was a column of large print in which a name stood out, in even larger characters. It was his name: Alex Barny.

There was another photograph, too, smaller: a guy with his arm around a woman with a baby in her arms. Alex cleared his throat and hawked onto the paper. His saliva, which had picked up a few traces of tobacco on its way, landed on the baby's face. He spat again, this time hitting his intended target, the face of a cop smiling at his little family. A cop who was now dead...

He emptied the rest of the beer over the paper, causing the ink to run, blurring the pictures and bloating the newsprint. For a few moments, he was lost in contemplation of the progressive staining of the pages by the trails of liquid. Then he stamped on the whole mess, reducing the paper to shreds.

A wave of anxiety flooded through him. His eyes misted over, but no tears came; the sobs that formed in his throat failed to materialize, leaving him distraught. He tidied up his dressing, rearranging the folds and tightening the whole thing by shifting the safety pin.

With his hands flat on his knees, he stayed where he was, staring into the night. During the first days after his arrival at the farmhouse, he had found it devilishly hard to adjust to the solitude. He had a slight fever because of his infected wound, and there was a buzzing in his ears that blended unpleasantly with the chirping of the cicadas. He scrutinized the garrigue, and often thought he detected movement in the scrub; night sounds filled him with alarm. His revolver was always in his hand or, when he lay down, on his stomach. He feared that he might go mad.

The bag full of banknotes lay at the foot of his bed. He would dangle his arm over the iron bedpost and plunge his hand among the wads of bills, turning them over, fondling, enjoying the feel of them.

He had moments of euphoria when he would suddenly burst out laughing and tell himself that after all nothing could happen to him. They would never find him. He was safe here. There were no other houses, no neighbors, for over a kilometer around. Even then, it was only some Dutch or German tourists who had bought up a ruined farmhouse for a vacation home. Some hippies with herds of goats. A potter. Nothing to fear! In the daytime, he occasionally observed the road and the vicinity through binoculars. The foreigners would take long walks, picking flowers. Their children were extraordinarily blond—two little girls and a boy slightly older. The mother would sunbathe naked on the flat roof of their house. Alex would spy on her, squeezing his crotch and grousing to himself...

❖

He went back inside and made himself an omelet, which he ate straight from the pan, mopping up the sloppy part with bread. Then he played darts, but the to-ing and fro-ing needed to retrieve the darts after each turn soon wore him out. There was also a pinball machine, which had worked when he arrived but had now been on the blink for a week.

He turned the television on. He couldn't make up his mind between a Western on France 3 and a variety show on Channel 1. The Western was about a bandit who became a judge after having terrorized an entire town. The guy was crazy—he went around with a bear—and his head was always strangely out of kilter. The fact was that this bandit-cum-judge was the survivor of a botched hanging...Alex muted the sound.

He had seen a judge once, a real one, complete with a red robe and a weird white fur collar. At the Hall of Justice in Paris. Vincent had dragged him there to witness the superior court in action. He was a little bit nuts, Vincent. He was also Alex's only real friend.

At present, Alex was in deep shit. Vincent, he thought, would have known what to do in this kind of situation: how to get out of this hole without getting caught by the cops, how to unload the bills, whose serial numbers were undoubtedly known, how to get to a foreign country, how to get oneself forgotten. Vincent spoke English, Spanish...

In the first place, Vincent would never have let himself be fooled so easily. He would have foreseen the cop—and the hidden camera in the ceiling that recorded all Alex's exploits. Some exploits! Beginning with his wild intrusion into the branch bank, yelling and pointing his revolver at the teller...

Vincent would have thought to check out the regular Monday customers—especially the cop, who was always off duty on Mondays and always withdrew cash at ten in the morning before going to do his shopping at the Carrefour supermarket nearby. Vincent would have worn a ski mask; he would have shot up the surveillance camera...Alex had worn a ski mask, as a matter of fact, but the cop had torn it off. Vincent would not have hesitated to shoot that guy who wanted to play the hero. If you were going to die...

But it was he, Alex—petrified, waiting for that fraction of a second too long instead of deciding to open fire instantly—who had allowed himself to be taken by surprise. It was he, Alex, who had taken the bullet in the thigh; he, Alex, who had dragged himself out of the bank streaming blood and clutching a bag stuffed with bills. No, there was no denying that Vincent would have done a far better job.

Vincent, though, was no longer around. No one knew where he was hiding. Perhaps he was dead? In any case, his absence had been a real catastrophe for Alex.

Still, Alex had learned. He had made new friends after Vincent vanished. One of them had even supplied him with false papers and this hideout in the middle of the scrubland of Provence. The almost four years since Vincent's disappearance had transformed Alex, and his father's farm with its tractor and its cows was very far off now. For a time, he had worked as a bouncer at a nightclub in Meaux, where his massive paws served to make short work, on many a Saturday night, of wine-besotted and unruly patrons. Alex soon had fine clothes, a large ring, his own car. Quite the big shot!

The more he beat people up for his employers, however, the more he came to feel that mugging a few on his own account would be no bad thing. So Alex mugged and mugged and mugged. He did so late at night, in the higher-class districts of Paris, as customers tumbled out of the clubs and restaurants. He garnered a rich harvest of wallets, more or less well filled, and plenty of the credit cards that came in so handy for maintaining his ever more lavish wardrobe.

But Alex grew tired of thumping people so hard and so often in exchange for what was after all a pathetic payoff. It would take just one bank job—a large-scale mugging, in effect—and he could be through with mugging for life...

He lay limply in an armchair, staring at a blank television screen. A mouse ran squeaking along the baseboard just inches from his hand. With a swift motion he straightened his arm, palm open, and his fingers closed over the small furry body. He could feel the tiny heart throbbing in fear. He remembered the fields, the wheels of the tractor startling the rats and birds concealed in the hedgerows.

He brought the animal close to his face and began to squeeze it gently. His nails dug into its silken coat. The squeaks became sharper. Then his gaze lighted upon the front page of the newspaper, on the boldface print, on his own image held prisoner by the columns of reporters' baloney.

He got to his feet, returned to the front steps of the house, and then with all his strength hurled the mouse away into the dark of the night.

There was that taste of mildewed earth in your mouth, all that mud underneath you, tepid and soft against your back (your shirt was ripped), that odor of moss and rotting wood. And then there was the vise of his hands around your neck and over your face, those iron fingers holding you fast, that knee braced against the small of your back and pressing down with the full weight of his body behind it, as though he wanted to force you down into the ground and make you disappear.

He was panting, trying to get his wind back. And you were not moving now—just waiting. The knife was nearby, in the grass somewhere to your right. He would surely be obliged, any moment now, to relax his grip. When he did, you could heave up, throw him off, get him off balance, grab the knife, and kill him, kill him—rip the bastard's belly open!

Who was he? A madman? A sadist on the prowl in the forest? For long seconds the two of you lay painfully entwined in the mire, husbanding your breath. Did he mean to kill you? To rape you and then kill you?

The forest was utterly silent, inert, devoid of life. He said nothing, breathing more easily now. You awaited some gesture— a hand, perhaps, moving to your groin. Something of that sort. Little by little you got control of your terror; you felt prepared to fight—to jab your fingers into his eyes, to find a place at his throat to bite. But nothing transpired. There you were, beneath his weight, waiting.

Then he laughed. A little laugh, joyful, ingenuous, juvenile. The laugh of a boy who has just been given a Christmas present. As the laugh ended, you heard his voice, composed, neutral.

"Don't be afraid, kid. Don't move. I'm not going to hurt you."

His left hand was removed from your throat, and the flashlight came on. The knife was there, sure enough, protruding from the grass just a few inches away. But, stamping down even harder on your wrist, he grabbed the weapon himself and flung it far away. Your last chance…

He set the flashlight down and, taking you by the hair, twisted your face into the beam of yellow light. You were blinded by it. He spoke once more:

"Yes, it's you, all right."

His knee ground ever harder into your back. You cried out, but he clamped a vaporous rag over your mouth. You fought not to succumb, but by the time his grip loosened a little, you were already dead to the world. A great bubbling torrent of blackness rolled over you.

It was a long time before you came back to your senses. Your memory was a fog. You had had a nightmare, a ghastly dream. Were you in your bed?

No, everything was dark, dark as deep sleep. But now you were well and truly awake. You screamed. A long, long scream. You tried to move, to get up.

But your wrists, your ankles were shackled. You could barely move at all. In the obscurity you felt the ground on which you lay. It was hard and covered with some kind of oilcloth. Behind you was a wall padded with moss. Your chains were anchored to it, and solidly. You pulled on them, bracing a foot against the wall, but clearly even a far greater traction than you could muster would have been equally ineffective.

Only then did you become aware of your nakedness. You were naked, completely naked, chained to a wall. Frenetically, you inspected your body for signs of wounds that might somehow be causing no pang. But your delicate skin was as intact as it was pain-free.

It was not cold in that dark room. Naked as you were, you felt no chill. You called, shouted, roared. Then you wept, beating your fists against the wall, rattling your chains, and screaming with impotent rage.

It seemed that you had been yelling for hours. You were sitting up on the floor, on the oilcloth. You wondered whether you had been drugged, whether all this was hallucination, delusion…Or perhaps you were dead—killed that night on your motorcycle? You could not recall an accident for the moment, but maybe memory would return? Was this what death was like: being chained up in the dark, knowing nothing?...

But no, you decided, you were alive. You started yelling again. The sadist had taken you captive in the forest, but for some reason he had done you no harm, none.

I have gone mad—that was another thought that came to you. Your voice was weak, broken, cracked; your throat was dry, and you could no longer shout.

Then you began to feel thirsty.

You slept. When you awoke, the thirst was still there, crouched in the shadows, lying in wait. It had kept vigil, patiently, as you slept. Now it gripped your throat, tenacious, perverse. It was a scratchy, thick dust that coated your mouth, a sand that grated between your teeth; not a simple desire to drink, but something quite different, something you had never experienced, something whose name itself, crisp and clear, resembled a whiplash: THIRST.

You strove to think of something else. You recited poems in your mind. Now and again you raised yourself and called for help, banging on the wall. You screamed: I'm thirsty; you moaned: I'm thirsty; at last you could only think: I'm thirsty! Groaning, you implored, you begged, that you be given something to drink. You regretted having urinated earlier, at the very beginning. You had pulled on your chains as hard as you could, trying to piss away from the patch of oilcloth that was all you had by way of a bed and keep it clean. I'll die of thirst, you thought, I should have drunk my piss...

You slept some more. Was it for hours—or just minutes? It was impossible to know, so long as you lay there naked in the dark, without any point of reference.

❖

A good deal of time had elapsed, however. Suddenly it dawned on you: it was all a mistake! You had been taken for someone else; it was not you that they wanted to torture like this. You mustered all your strength, then screamed:

"Monsieur, I beg of you! Come here! You have made a mistake! I am Vincent Moreau! You made a mistake! Vincent Moreau! Vincent Moreau!"

And then you remembered the flashlight in the forest—the beam of yellow light on your face, and his voice, expressionless, saying, "It's you, all right."

Okay, so it was you.

II

The Poison

1

Richard Lafargue rose early that Monday morning. His day would be busy. He went straight to the pool and swam a few laps, then took his breakfast on the lawn, enjoying the early morning sunshine as he absently scanned the headlines of the daily papers.

Roger was waiting for him at the wheel of the Mercedes. Before leaving, though, he paid a visit to Eve, who was still asleep. He slapped her gently awake. She sat straight up, startled. The sheet slipped aside, and Richard noticed the graceful curve of her breasts. With the tip of his forefinger he caressed her, tracing a path from her ribcage to the point of her nipple.

She could not help laughing; she seized his hand and drew it to her belly. Richard flinched. Straightening up, he started for the door. Once there, he turned. Eve had tossed the sheet off altogether and held out welcoming arms. It was his turn to laugh.

"Bastard!" she hissed. "You're dying for it!"

He shrugged, turned on his heel, and disappeared.

Half an hour later, he was at the hospital in the center of Paris where he ran an internationally renowned plastic surgery department. But he spent only his mornings there and devoted his afternoons to a private clinic he owned in Boulogne.

He shut himself in his office to study the file on an

operation scheduled for that day. His assistants waited impatiently. After taking the time he needed to think the case over, he donned scrubs and headed for the operating room.

The room was surmounted by a glassed-in gallery with tiered seating. Today there was a goodly number of spectators, doctors and students. They listened attentively to Lafargue's voice, distorted by the loudspeakers, as he expounded the procedure.

"Well, what we have here, on forehead and cheeks, are large keloid plaques, the result of burns from the explosion of volatile chemicals. The nasal pyramid is virtually nonexistent, the eyelids have been destroyed. You are looking at perfect indications for treatment by means of tubular skin flaps. We shall be drawing for this purpose upon both the arm and the abdomen."

With the help of a scalpel, Lafargue was already cutting large rectangles of skin from the patient's stomach. Above him, the spectators' faces pressed against the glass. An hour later he was able to show a first result: skin flaps sown into tubes had left the subject's arm and abdomen and been grafted to his burn-ravaged face. Doubly anchored, they would serve to rebuild the completely ruinous facial integument.

The patient was wheeled out. Lafargue removed his surgical mask and finished his commentary.

"In this case, the plan of action was determined by what needed the most urgent attention. It goes without saying that this sort of intervention will have to be repeated a number of times before a fully satisfactory outcome can be achieved."

He thanked his audience for their attention and left

the operating room. It was past noon. Lafargue set off for a nearby restaurant. On the way, he happened to pass a perfumery. He went in and bought a bottle of scent, intending to present it to Eve that evening.

After lunch, Roger drove him to Boulogne. His visiting hours began at two. Lafargue hurried his patients along: a young mother and her son and his harelip, and a whole raft of noses—Monday was the day for noses: broken noses, overlarge noses, deviated noses...Lafargue palpated faces to left and right of the septum and showed before-and-after photographs. Most of his patients were women, but he saw a few men, too.

When the consultations were over, he worked on his own, catching up on the latest American journals. Roger came for him at six.

Once back at Le Vésinet, he knocked on Eve's door and slid back the bolts. She was seated at the piano naked, playing a sonata, and she seemed not to register Richard's presence. At the piano stool, she kept her back to him. Locks of her curly black hair bounced on her shoulders, her head bobbing as her fingers struck the keyboard. He admired the flesh and the muscles of her back, the dimples at its base, her buttocks...Without warning, she abandoned the light, fluid sonata and launched into the tune Richard so hated. She hummed along in a throaty voice, stressing the low notes: "Some day, he'll come along, the man I love..." Then she deliberately hit a wrong note, stopped playing, and span the stool around with a twist of her hips. She sat facing Richard, her thighs apart, her fists on her knees, in an attitude of obscene defiance.

For a few moments he was unable to take his eyes off

the dark fleece that covered her pubis. She frowned, and then with deliberation spread her legs even wider and slid a finger into the fissure of her sex, separating the labia and moaning.

"Stop it!" Richard shouted.

Gauchely, he proffered the bottle of perfume he had bought that morning. She looked him over sardonically. He placed the gift on the piano and tossed her a robe, demanding that she cover herself.

Batting it aside, she leaped to her feet and ran to him all smiles, pressing herself against him. She wrapped her arms around Richard's neck and rubbed her breasts against his torso. He was forced to twist her wrists to get free.

"Get ready!" he ordered her. "It's been a magnificent day. We're going out."

"Should I dress like a whore?"

He went for her, taking her by the throat with one hand and holding her away from him. He repeated his order. But she was in pain and suffocating, and he had to release her immediately.

"I'm sorry," he mumbled. "But please, please, get dressed."

He went back down to the ground floor, anxious. To calm himself, he decided to look at his mail. He hated having to deal with the material details of household management, but after Eve's arrival he had been obliged to discharge the person he had previously relied on to handle the minor paperwork.

He worked on the overtime due Roger and on Lise's upcoming paid days off, but he got the hourly wage wrong and had to start over again. He was still poring over his papers when Eve appeared in the drawing room.

She was stunning in a low-necked black lamé dress, a

string of pearls about her throat. When she leaned over him, her pallid skin was redolent with the perfume he had just given her.

She smiled at him and took his arm. He got behind the wheel of the Mercedes, and a few minutes later they were walking side by side in the forest of Saint-Germain, which was full of strollers attracted by the mildness of the evening.

She had her head on his shoulder. They didn't speak for a time, and then he told her about his operation of that morning.

"You're boring the shit out of me!" She spoke in a singsong voice.

He fell silent, a little vexed. She had taken his hand and was watching him in apparent amusement. She made for a bench.

"Richard?"

He seemed distracted. She had to call his name again. He came and sat next to her.

"I'd like to see the sea. It's been such a long time. I used to love swimming, you know. A day—just one. Let's go and see the sea. I'll do whatever you want, after..."

He shrugged, explaining that that wasn't the problem.

"I promise you I won't run off."

"Your promises are worthless! Anyway, you already do whatever I want."

With a gesture of irritation, he asked her to be quiet. They walked a little more, as far as the water's edge. Young people were windsurfing on the Seine.

"I'm hungry!" she announced, and waited for Richard's response. He offered to take her to supper at a restaurant not far away.

❖

They chose a table on a leafy terrace. A waiter came and took their order. Eve ate heartily; Richard barely touched his food. She had the greatest difficulty getting a spiny lobster tail out of its shell and in frustration produced a little-girl tantrum. He could not help laughing at her. She joined in, and Richard's features froze. My God, he thought, there are moments when she seems almost happy! It's incredible—and unfair!

Perceiving the change in Lafargue's attitude, she decided to put the situation to good use. She gestured for him to lean over to her, then whispered in his ear.

"Richard, listen. That waiter, over there, he hasn't been able to take his eyes off me since the beginning of the meal. I could arrange things for later..."

"Shut up!"

"But I'm serious. I can go to the toilet, make a rendezvous with him, and have him screw me later, in the bushes."

He had drawn away from her, but she went on whispering, more loudly now, and laughing derisively.

"So you don't want to? If you hide, you can watch everything. I'll make sure to get us close to you. Look at him—he's positively drooling!"

He blew cigarette smoke full into her face. But she didn't stop.

"No? Really? Not like that, the quick in-and-out. I'd just lift up my dress...You used to like that, though, at the beginning, didn't you?"

And it was true: "at the beginning," Richard would take Eve into the park, the Bois de Vincennes or the Bois de Boulogne, and make her offer herself to men on the prowl. Then he would observe her humiliation from the cover of a hedge. But later, for fear of getting caught in a police sweep, which would have been catastrophic, he had rented the studio apartment in Rue Godot-de-Mauroy. There he prostituted Eve on a regular basis two or three times a month. This sufficed to assuage his loathing.

"You're determined to be insufferable today, aren't you, my dear? I'm almost sorry for you."

"I don't believe you."

She is provoking me, he thought. She would have me believe she is quite happy to be in the slime where I force her to live. She wants me to think she gets pleasure from degrading herself.

Eve kept up her act, even risking a wink at the waiter, who turned as red as a turkey cock.

"Come on, we're going now. We've had quite enough of that. If you are so keen to 'please me,' we can go tomorrow for your appointments, or maybe I'll even ask you to do a little streetwalking..."

Eve smiled and took his hand so as not to lose face; but he knew perfectly well how mortifying all those metered encounters were for her and how much she suffered every time he made her sell herself: sometimes, through the one-way mirror in the studio apartment, he saw her eyes welling with tears and her face contorted as she strove to contain her distress. At such moments he reveled in this suffering, which was his only comfort.

They returned to the house at Le Vésinet. Eve ran across the grounds, undressed swiftly, and dived into the pool with a cry of joy. She splashed about in the water, disappearing beneath the surface for quick breath-holding bursts.

When she climbed out of the pool, Lafargue wrapped her in a large Turkish towel and vigorously rubbed her dry. She let him do it, staring up at the stars. Then he walked her up to her flat, where, as on every other evening, she stretched out on the rush mat. He busied himself with the pipe and the balls of opium, and brought the drug to her.

"Richard," she murmured, "you really are the biggest bastard I have ever met…"

He made sure that she finished her daily dose. He need not have bothered: she had been missing it sorely for some time already.

After thirst came hunger. To the dryness of your throat, to the feeling that sharp-edged stones were ripping at your mouth, were added deep, diffuse pains in your belly, like hands wrenching at your stomach, filling it with bile and making it cramp horribly.

For days now (and the pain was so bad, it must surely be days), you had been crouching in your hole. But it was more than a hole, in fact, for it seemed to you, though you had no way of being certain, that the place where you were held captive was vast. The echo of your cries off the walls and eyes now accustomed to the dark almost convinced you that you could see the boundaries of your prison.

You raved continually, hour after interminable hour. Slumped on your litter, you no longer sat up. From time to time you raged against your shackles, biting at the metal and producing little growls, like some wild animal.

Once, long ago, you had seen a film, a documentary on hunting, with pitiful images of a fox, its paw in a trap, tearing at its own flesh, ripping it off in shreds, until the trap's grip was loose enough for the beast to free itself and make off, mutilated.

But you could not bite at your wrists or ankles. They were bloody, nevertheless, from the incessant chafing between skin and metal. The flesh was hot, swollen. Had you still been rational, you would have feared gangrene, infection, the decay that, starting from your extremities, could invade your entire body.

But you dreamed only of water, rushing torrents, pouring rain—anything at all that could be drunk. You urinated with the greatest difficulty, and each time the pain in your back would be more violent. There would be a burning sensation running down through your penis, but only a few drops of hot piss would dribble forth. You sprawled in your own excrement; dried plaques of shit stuck to your skin.

Oddly, your sleep was untroubled. You slept profoundly, felled by fatigue, but your awakenings were atrocious and accompanied by hallucinations. Monstrous creatures lay in wait for you in the dark, ready to pounce and sink their teeth into you. You thought you heard claws scratching at the cement; you thought you saw the yellow eyes of rats in the shadows, watching you.

You called out for Alex, but your cry emerged as a scraping sound in your throat. If only Alex were there, he would have freed you from your chains. Alex would have known what to do. He would have come up with a solution, employed some peasant ruse. Alex! He should have been looking for you since you disappeared. Which was how long ago now? HOW LONG?

And then HE came. One day—or one night, for there was no way of telling. A door—right across from you—was opened: a rectangle of light that blinded you at first.

The door closed once more, but HE had entered. His presence filled your prison.

You held your breath, listened for the merest sound, and crouched motionless against the wall like a terrified cockroach caught in a sudden glare. You might as well have been an insect captured by a bloated spider and kept on hand for an eventual meal, when she would savor you at her leisure, whenever the whim arose to taste your blood. You pictured her furry legs, her great bulbous merciless eyes, her soft belly gorged with meat, throbbing, spongy, and her venomous jaws, her black maw preparing to suck the life out of you.

All at once you were dazzled by a powerful spotlight. There you lay, sole actor in the drama of your imminent death, ready for the last act. You made out a figure, a silhouette seated in an armchair ten or twelve feet in front of you. But you could not discern the monster's features, lost in the blackness behind the light. He had crossed his legs and clasped his hands under his chin; he was contemplating you motionlessly.

You made a superhuman effort to get up and, on your knees, your hands palm to palm as though in prayer, you pleaded for something to drink. The words became jumbled on their way out of your mouth. Stretching your arms out toward him, you begged.

He did not respond. You stammered your name: Vincent Moreau, monsieur. There's been a mistake, monsieur. I am Vincent Moreau. You passed out.

When you came around, he was gone. Then the true meaning of despair was borne in upon you. The spotlight was still on you. You saw your body, the pus-filled boils, the streaked dirt, the skin rubbed raw by the shackles, the crusted shit on your thighs, the long fingernails.

The violent white light made you weep. Another good stretch of time passed before he came back. Once again he sat down in the armchair facing you. At his feet he had placed an object that you identified instantly. A pitcher! Water? You were on your knees, on all fours, head bowed. He approached you. He poured the water in the pitcher over your head, all at once. You lapped at the puddle forming on the floor. You stroked your hair with trembling hands to squeeze out the moisture, which you licked from your palms.

He went and refilled the pitcher and handed it to you. Avidly, you drank the contents down in a single draft. Then a searing *pain shot through your stomach, and from your nether end spurted a long stream of diarrhea. He watched you. You did not turn to the wall or seek to evade his gaze. Squatting at his feet, you relieved yourself, happy simply to have drunk. You were nothing now—nothing but an animal, thirsty, hungry, and battered. An animal that had once been Vincent Moreau.*

He laughed. The little childish laugh you had heard before, in the forest.

He came back often with water. His figure still seemed immense to you behind the spotlight. His enormous menacing shadow filled the room. But you were no longer afraid, for he gave you water, and you read this as a sign that he meant to keep you alive.

Later, he brought you a tin bowl containing a reddish broth with meatballs floating in it. He plunged one hand into the bowl, grabbing your hair and pulling your head back with the other. You ate from his hand, sucked on his sauce-slick fingers. It was good. He left you to finish the food by yourself, flat on your belly, your face plunged into the bowl. Soon not a trace of the swill that your master had brought you was to be seen.

Day after day, the soup was always the same. Your jailer would come in, give you the bowl and the pitcher, and watch you guzzle. Then he would leave, always with the little laugh.

You regained your strength by degrees. You set a little water aside to wash with and always eased yourself at the same place, beyond the edge of the oilcloth.

Insidiously, hope was returning: your master wanted you...

Alex started violently. The sound of a car engine had intruded upon the silence of the garrigue. He consulted his watch: seven in the morning. He yawned. His mouth was dry, his tongue thick from the alcohol—beer followed by gin—that he had imbibed during the night before getting to sleep.

He grabbed the binoculars and focused on the road. The Dutch tourist family at full complement had packed themselves into a Land Rover, the kids clutching buckets and spades. A day at the seaside in prospect. The young mother wore a bikini, and her heavy breasts strained at the thin material of the swimsuit. Alex was suffering from a morning erection. How long was it since he had been with a woman? Six weeks or more? Yes, the last time had been a farm girl. A distant memory now.

Her name was Annie, a friend from childhood. He could see her still, her red hair in braids, playing in the schoolyard. In another life, almost forgotten: the life of Alex the klutz, Alex the hayseed. Just before the bank hold-up, he had paid a visit to his parents. No doubt about *their* still being hicks!

He had driven into their farmyard one rainy afternoon in his car, a Ford with a roaring engine. His father stood waiting for him on the front steps. Alex felt proud of his clothes, his shoes, his new-man appearance with every last whiff of the soil gone.

He made a bit of a face at first, the father. Playing the village bullyboy as a nightclub bouncer did not seem to him like much of a trade. Still, it must pay well—you only had to look at the kid's outfit! Alex's manicured hands and fingernails were not lost on the older man, either, and he broke into a smile of welcome.

The two of them had sat facing each other in the main room. The father had brought out the customary bread, the salami, the pâté, and the liter of red and started eating. Alex merely lit a cigarette, ignoring the mustard glass of wine that had been poured for him. The mother contemplated them in silence without taking a seat. Louis and René, the farm boys, were there, too. What could they talk about? The weather they were having? The weather they were about to have? Before long, Alex got up, gave his father an affectionate punch on the shoulder, and went out onto the village's main street. Window curtains were discreetly pulled aside as the locals took a furtive look at the Barnys' boy, the bad one, as he went by.

Alex went into the Café des Sports and, just showing off, bought everyone a round. A few old men were playing cards, thumping loudly on the table as they laid out their hands, and two or three youngsters pushed and shoved one another at a pinball machine. Alex was delighted with the impression he made. He shook hands with everyone and drank to the health of one and all.

Back in the street, he passed Madame Moreau, Vincent's mother. She was a good-looking woman, tall, graceful, and well turned out. Or rather, she had been—for right after her son's disappearance she had fallen apart, withered, and taken to dressing sloppily at all times. She slouched and dragged her feet as she made her way to the minimarket to do her shopping.

Every week, as regular as clockwork, Madame Moreau paid a ritual visit to the police station in Meaux in search of news of her missing son. All hope of finding him had been abandoned four years ago now. She had placed notices in all the papers, with Vincent's photo, to no avail. The police had told her that there were thousands of disappearances in France every year, and most of the time no trace of the missing person was ever found. Vincent's bike was in the garage; the police had returned it to her after a thorough examination. The fingerprints on it were Vincent's. The machine had been found lying on an embankment with its front wheel buckled and no gas in the tank. A search of the forest around had turned up nothing.

Alex spent that night in the village. It was Saturday, and there was a dance. Annie was there, her hair as red as ever, her limbs a little thicker. She worked at the bean cannery in the next village over. Alex danced a slow number with her, then took her walking in the woods nearby. They made love in his car, lying uncomfortably on its reclining seats.

The next day, after kissing his folks goodbye, Alex left. Eight days later, he held up the Crédit Agricole branch and killed the cop. Everyone in the village must have clipped the front page of the paper with Alex's picture on it, along with the picture of the cop and his family.

Alex unrolled his bandage: his wound was inflamed, its edges bright red. He sprinkled his thigh with the powder his friend had given him, then bound himself up again, pulling the bandage good and tight over the fresh dressing.

His hard-on was still there, almost painful itself. He masturbated furiously, thinking about Annie. He had never had a lot of girls. He usually had to pay them. It had been much better when Vincent was around. Vincent had chicks falling all over him in droves. They often went to dances, the two of them. Vincent would dance; he would get every cool girl from miles around to dance with him. Alex used to sit at the bar and drink beer. Watching Vincent doing his number. Vincent smiled at the girls with his great smile. It had them eating out of his hand. There was a motion of the head he had, cute, a sort of come-on, and then his hands would be roving up and down his partner's back, from her thighs to her shoulders, caressing her. He would bring girls over to the bar and introduce them to Alex.

If things worked out, Alex would go with the girl after Vincent, but things didn't always work out. Some of them simply couldn't help putting on airs and graces. And they didn't always like Alex, who was muscular, hairy as an ape, and very solidly built. No, they would rather have Vincent—puny, hairless, delicate Vincent with his oh-so-pretty face!

Lost in thoughts of an earlier time, Alex jerked off. Laboriously mobilizing his shaky memory, he tried to pass all the girls he had shared with Vincent in rapid review. And to think that Vincent had abandoned him! The bastard! He was probably in America by now, getting laid by starlets!

A naked calendar girl adorned the whitewashed wall next to Alex's bed. He closed his eyes as warm creamy sperm flowed into his hand. He wiped himself off with a spare dressing and went down to the kitchen to make coffee. He made it very strong. As the water was heating, he thrust his head under the tap, pushing aside the piles of dirty dishes that cluttered the sink.

He sipped from his steaming bowl of coffee and chewed on the remains of a sandwich. Outside, it was already stifling, the sun now high in the sky. Alex turned the radio on and listened to a quiz show on Radio Luxembourg called *The Suitcase*. He didn't give a shit about the show, but he enjoyed hearing the losers getting the answers wrong and failing to collect the money they wanted so much.

He didn't give a shit because he had not lost the money. In *his* suitcase—which wasn't so much a suitcase, more a bag—were four million francs. A fortune. He had counted the wads of bills, over and over. New, crackling bills. He had looked in the dictionary to see who these people were whose likenesses were printed on the notes: Voltaire, Pascal, Berlioz. How weird, to have your photo on a banknote—rather like being turned into a bit of money yourself.

He stretched out on the couch and returned to his pastime, a jigsaw with more than two thousand pieces. A château in the Valley of the Loire: Langeais. He was close to getting it done. In the attic, the first day, he had come across several Heller model kits, complete with glue, paint, and decals. So he had built Stukas and Spitfires, as well as a car—a 1935 Hispano-Suiza. They all stood on the floor now, mounted on their plastic bases and carefully painted. When he ran out of kits, Alex built a model of his parents' farm: the two main buildings, the outbuildings, the fences. By gluing matches together he achieved a clumsy, naive, touching replica. All that was missing was the tractor, so he cut one out of a piece of cardboard. Later, on a return visit to the attic, he turned up the jigsaw puzzle...

The farmhouse where he was hiding out belonged to a friend of his, a guy he had met working as a nightclub bouncer. You could spend a few weeks there without fear of unannounced visits from curious neighbors. The friend had also supplied him with a phony identity card, but Alex's now notorious face was liable to be displayed in every police station in France, and in the "most wanted" section, to boot. The cops hate it when one of their own gets killed.

The pieces of the puzzle obstinately refused to fit together. Alex was working on part of the sky. It was all blue, very hard to do. The château's turrets, the drawbridge—all that had been easy, but the sky was another matter. Cloudless and empty, it was very tricky. Alex got irritated, which made him try even more unlikely joins; he was continually assembling patches of sky only to pull them apart again.

On the floor, just near the board on which he had laid out the jigsaw, crawled a spider. A squat and repulsive spider. She picked a corner of the wall and set about spinning a web. The thread flowed continually from her rounded abdomen. She came and went carefully and laboriously. With a match, Alex set fire to the just-completed portion of her web. The spider panicked, checking her surroundings, looking out for the advent of some enemy; but since the concept of matches was not inscribed in her genes, she soon went back to work.

She spun tirelessly, joining up her thread, anchoring it to rough spots on the wall, making use of every splinter of wood in the floor. Alex found a dead mosquito and tossed it into the newly constructed web. The spider rushed over, circled this carrion, but disdained it. Alex divined the reason for her lack of interest: the mosquito was already dead. Hobbling, he went out to the front steps, delicately gathered up a moth hiding under a tile, and placed it in the web.

The moth struggled to escape the viscous toils. The spider promptly reappeared, turning the prey this way and that before weaving a cocoon for it and storing the insect in a crack in the wall, safe for a future feast.

Eve was sitting at her dressing table, examining her face in the mirror. A childish face, with great sad almond-shaped eyes. Touching her index finger softly to the skin of her jaw, she felt the hardness of the bone, the sharpness of the chin, the relief of the teeth through the fleshy mass of the lips.

Her cheekbones were prominent and her nose turned up; it was a delicately shaped, perfectly rounded nose.

She turned her head slightly, tipped the mirror, and was herself surprised by the strange expression that her reflection had elicited. There was almost too much perfection, and such radiant charm created a sort of malaise in her. She had never known a man who could resist her attraction or remain indifferent to her glance. No man could pierce her aura of mystery or pin down the quality that invested her every gesture with an enrapturing ambiguity. She drew them all to her, piquing their interest, arousing their desire, playing on the tension they felt once in her presence.

The outward signs of this seductiveness filled her with an ambivalent calm: she would have liked to repel them, put them to flight, free herself of them, provoke repugnance in them; and yet the fascination she exercised without wanting it was her only revenge, paltry in its very infallibility.

She made herself up, then took the easel from its case and spread out the paints and brushes and resumed work on a canvas that she had in hand. It was a portrait of Richard, vulgar and crudely executed. She showed him seated on a bar stool with legs apart, cross-dressed as a woman, a cigarette-holder in his mouth, wearing a pink dress and black stockings held up by a garter-belt; his feet were crammed into high-heeled shoes.

He was smiling beatifically, even idiotically. Grotesque falsies made of old rags hung pathetically over his flaccid belly. Painted with obsessive precision, the face was covered with red blotches. No viewer of the picture could have failed to supply a voice for this pathetic, monstrous caricature: the rasping croak of a broken-down fishwife.

❖

No, your master had not killed you. Later, you came to regret it.
For the moment, he was treating you better. He would come and
give you showers, spraying you with tepid water from a garden
hose, even letting you have a piece of soap.

The spotlight stayed on all the time. The darkness had given
way to its blinding light, artificial, cold, and incessant.

For hours at a time your master would stay with you,
sitting in an armchair opposite you, scrutinizing your slightest
movement.

At the start of these "observation" sessions, you dared say
nothing, for fear of arousing his ire, for fear that at night thirst
and hunger would return to punish you for this crime whose
nature was still a mystery to you but which you were apparently
doomed to expiate.

But then you got your courage up. Timidly, you asked him
what the date was, to find out how long you had been locked
up here. He replied immediately, smiling: the twenty-third
of October. So, he had been holding you captive for over two
months. Two months of being hungry and thirsty—and how
long eating from his hand, licking that tin plate, lying prostrate
at his feet, being washed with a hose?

You wept then, asked why he was doing all this to you. This time
he said nothing. You could see his face, which was impenetrable,
crowned by white hair: a face with a certain nobility about it—a
face that, possibly, you had seen somewhere before.

He kept coming into your prison and staying there, sitting
before you, impassive. He would disappear only to return a
little later. The nightmares of your early days of incarceration
were gone. Could he be slipping tranquilizers into your rations?
True, your anxiety was still there, but its object had changed.
You were sure of staying alive, for otherwise, you reasoned, he
would have killed you already. His intent was not to let you

slowly agonize, shrivel up, and die. It was, therefore, something else...

A little later, your meal routine was changed. Your master set up a folding table and a stool for you. He gave you a plastic knife and fork like the ones they give you on airplanes. A plate replaced the tin bowl. And real meals soon followed: fruit, vegetables, cheese. You took enormous pleasure in eating as you mulled over your memories of the first days.

You were still chained up, but your master cared for the abrasions on your wrists caused by the shackles. You would spread cream on the sores, and he would wind an elastic bandage round your wrist beneath the steel cuffs.

Everything was going better, but still he said nothing. You told your life story. He listened with the greatest interest. His silence was intolerable to you. You had to talk, to tell and retell your stories, to recount your childhood, to stupefy yourself with words, merely to prove to him that you were not an animal!

Later still, your diet was suddenly improved once more. Now you were entitled to wine, to refined dishes that he must have had delivered by a caterer. The tableware was luxurious. Chained to your wall, naked as ever, you stuffed yourself with caviar, salmon, sorbets, and fancy pastries.

He sat beside you, serving you the food. He brought in a cassette player, and you listened to Chopin and Liszt.

As for the humiliating issue of the calls of nature, there too he became more humane, providing a conveniently placed waste bucket.

A time came at last when he allowed you to leave the wall at certain times. He released you from your fetters and led you around the cellar on a leash. You wandered slowly in a circle, round and round the spotlight.

To make the time pass more quickly, your master brought books. Classics: Balzac, Stendhal...In high school you had hated such works, but now, alone in your hole, sitting cross-legged on your patch of oilcloth or leaning your elbows on the folding table, you devoured them.

Little by little, your leisure took on substance. Your master took care to vary its pleasures. A stereo system appeared, complete with records; even an electronic chess set. Soon the time began to fly by. He had adjusted the brightness of the spotlight so that it no longer dazzled you, hanging a rag over the bulb to subdue the glare. The cellar filled with shadows, including your own, multiplied.

By virtue of all these changes, the absence of any brutality from your master, and the increasing luxury that gradually offset your solitude, you began to forget or at least to repress your fear. Your nakedness and the chains that still held you became an incongruity.

The walks around on the leash continued. You were a cultivated, intelligent beast. You suffered from memory lapses; at times you became acutely aware of the unreality, even the absurdity of your predicament. Of course, you had a burning desire for answers from your master, but he discouraged all questions, concerning himself exclusively with your material comfort. What would you like for supper? Did you enjoy the recording? And so on.

What about your village? Your mother? Weren't people searching for you? The faces of your friends were fading from your memory, melding into a thick fog. You could no longer recall Alex's features or the color of his hair. You talked to yourself a lot; you would catch yourself humming children's songs. Your distant past returned in violent and chaotic waves; images from your long-forgotten childhood would reemerge unannounced in startling clarity, only to dissipate in their turn into a vague mist.

Time itself expanded and contracted alarmingly. A minute, two hours, ten years?—you no longer knew the difference.

Your master noticed how this troubled you and gave you an alarm clock. You began to count the hours, avidly watching the progress of the hands on the clock. Time itself was a fiction: what did it matter if it was ten in the morning or ten at night? No, the important thing was that now you could once again regulate your life: at noon I am hungry, at midnight I am tired. A rhythm: something to hang on to.

Several more weeks had gone by. Among your master's gifts, you had found a pad of paper, pencils, and an eraser. You had begun to draw, clumsily at first, until your old facility returned. You sketched faceless portraits, mouths, confused landscapes, the ocean, immense cliffs, a giant hand creating waves. You scotch-taped these drawings to the wall; they helped you forget the bare concrete beneath.

In your head you had given your master a name. You dared not pronounce it in his presence, needless to say. You called him "Mygale," in memory of your past terrors. "Mygale"—a feminine-sounding name, the name of a repulsive animal that corresponded neither to his sex nor to the great refinement he displayed when choosing gifts for you.

But "Mygale," nevertheless, because he was just like a spider, slow and secretive, cruel and ferocious, obsessed yet impenetrable in his designs, hidden somewhere in this dwelling where he had held you captive for months: this luxury web, this gilded cage where he was the jailer and you the prisoner.

You had given up weeping and complaining. There was no pain in your new life in the material sense. At this time of year—February? March?—you would normally have been in high school, in your final year; instead, here you were, a captive in this concrete cubicle. You were habituated to your nudity. Shame was long gone. Only your chains were still intolerable.

It was probably some time in May, according to your reckoning, but possibly it was earlier, when a strange event occurred.

Your alarm said it was two-thirty in the afternoon. Mygale came down to visit you. He sat down in the armchair, as was his wont, to observe you. You were drawing. He got up and came over to you. You got to your feet and faced him standing up.

Your two faces were almost touching. You looked into his blue eyes, the only thing moving in his fixed and inscrutable countenance. Mygale raised his hand and placed it on your shoulder. Thence, with trembling fingers, he traced a path all the way up your neck. He felt your cheeks, your nose, gently pinching the skin.

Your heart was beating wildly. His hand, which felt hot, wandered back down over your chest, became soft and agile as it slid across your ribs, your belly. He fondled your muscles and stroked your smooth, hairless skin. Mistaking the meaning of these motions, you gauchely attempted a caress of your own, touching his face. Mygale slapped you violently, teeth clenched. He ordered you to turn around, then methodically continued his examination for several more minutes.

When it was over, you sat down, rubbing your cheek, which still smarted from his blow. He shook his head and laughed, running his fingers through your hair. You smiled.

Mygale left. You did not know what to make of this new kind of contact—a revolution, really, in your relationship. But the effort to think about it filled you with anxiety and called for a mental energy that had long been unavailable to you.

You resumed your drawing and stopped thinking about anything.

2

Alex had abandoned his jigsaw. He had gone out into the garden and was carving a piece of wood, an olive-tree root. As his knife hewed at the dry mass, as shaving after shaving fell to the ground, a crude but unmistakable form slowly emerged, that of a woman's body. Alex wore a broad straw hat to protect him from the sun. With a beer close to hand, he forgot his injury and lost himself in his painstaking task. For the first time in a very long while, he felt relaxed.

The telephone ringing made him start violently. He almost cut himself with the point of his Opinel knife, dropped the olive root and listened, transfixed. Hardly believing his ears, he ran into the farmhouse and planted himself before the phone, his arms dangling. Who could possibly know that he was here?

He grabbed his revolver—the Colt that he had taken from the cop's dead body. The weapon was more sophisticated than his own. Trembling, he picked up the receiver. Perhaps it was a local merchant or the post office, something stupid like that—even a wrong number!

He knew the voice. It was the former legionnaire at whose house he had found refuge after the robbery at the Crédit Agricole. Against a tidy consideration, the guy had contrived to treat Alex himself. There had been no need to extract the bullet, because it had exited from his thigh after passing through the quadriceps. He had given Alex antibiotics and dressed his wound after sewing it up in makeshift fashion. It hurt a lot, but the legionnaire swore up and down that he knew enough to do without a doctor. In any event, Alex had no choice: he was wanted by the police and would never get away otherwise. The normal course, outpatient treatment from a hospital, was out of the question.

The phone conversation was brief and staccato. The owner of the farmhouse was implicated in a sordid business connected with prostitution. The police were liable to show up at the door in the next few hours armed with a search warrant. Alex must clear out immediately...

He agreed, stammering out his thanks. The caller hung up. Alex paced up and down with the Colt still in his hand. He wept with rage. It was all about to start again: flight, pursuit, terror of being caught, tingling of the spine at the merest glimpse of a policeman's kepi.

He packed up quickly, transferring the money to a suitcase. He dressed in a cotton suit that he had found in a wardrobe. It was a little baggy, but what did that matter? The bandage around his thigh made a lump under the material. Freshly shaved, he tossed a bag into the trunk of the car: a change of clothes, toilet articles, not much else. There was no reason why the car should show up on police files: it was a Citroën CX, rented for a couple more months, and according to the legionnaire all its papers were in order.

Stowing the Colt in the glove compartment, Alex started the car. He left the iron gates to the property wide open behind him. On the road, he passed the Dutch family on their way back from the beach.

The major roads were swarming with vacationers in

their cars and police setting speed traps wherever they could find the slightest cover.

Alex was sweating profusely. His false papers would not withstand anything like serious scrutiny, for the simple reason that his picture was on file with the police.

He had to get up to Paris as quickly as possible. Once there, it would be easier for him to find a new bolt-hole until the police got over their fury and his wound was completely healed up. Then he would need to figure out how best to get out of the country without getting himself picked up at the border. But where would he go? Alex had no idea. He recalled whispered conversations among his "friends." Latin America was supposed to be a safe place. But one couldn't trust anybody. The money, he realized, would attract all kinds of people. Weakened by his injury, panic-stricken, and caught up in an adventure that it was beyond his capacities to confront, Alex sensed obscurely that the future would be no bed of roses.

He was terrified by the mere thought of prison. That time when Vincent had got him to go to the Paris Hall of Justice to attend the superior court had left him with a most agonizing memory that he simply could not shake off: the accused rearing up in the dock after the guilty verdict and letting out a long howl when he heard the sentence. In his nightmares Alex still saw the man's face, horribly contorted by incredulity and pain. He resolved to save a bullet for himself if ever he was caught.

He returned to Paris by back roads; the major arteries and highways were bound to be patrolled by the national security police at this, the height of the vacation season.

He had only one place to go: the house of the ex-legionnaire who had already helped him in his desperate flight from the fiasco at the bank. The man now ran a private surveillance company. Alex had no illusions about his savior's motives: he obviously had his eye on the money but was in no great hurry to make a move. If things smoothed out for Alex, if the bills were negotiable, then everything became possible...Meanwhile, the legionnaire knew that Alex was entirely dependent on him, not only to get over his injury but also to get out of the country. Alex, all at sea in his new life, was not about to throw himself blindly into the waiting arms of Interpol.

Alex had no foreign contacts offering him a guarantee of security abroad. He could easily foresee the moment when his protector would state his price for arranging a clean disappearance, complete with a credible passport and a quiet, discreet hideaway. And that price would certainly be a very high percentage of the proceeds of the hold-up...

Alex dwelt on his abiding hatred for men at ease in well-cut clothes, casually elegant, who knew how to talk to women. He himself was still a peasant, a rube that anybody could manipulate at will.

He wound up in a small suburban detached house at Livry-Gargan, one of the residential zones of Seine-Saint-Denis. After setting Alex up there, the legionnaire ordered him not to go out, and, much as at the farmhouse, he found a freezer stuffed to bursting, a bed, and a television set.

Alex made himself as comfortable as he could, using just one room. The neighboring houses were either unoccupied, in the process of being rented, or inhabited by bank employees with well-regulated lives who rose very early and returned only in the early evening. Moreover, the summer season meant that the Paris suburbs had been depopulated since the beginning of August. Alex took his ease, somewhat calmed by the emptiness that surrounded him. The legionnaire insisted absolutely on his remaining inside. Alex would not see his protector again until he returned to town in September, so Alex was to take things quietly until then. All he had to do was watch television, prepare frozen meals, take naps, and play solitaire...

3

Richard Lafargue was being visited by the sales representative of a Japanese pharmaceutical firm that had developed a new variety of the silicone commonly used in plastic surgery for breast augmentation. He listened attentively as the petty bureaucrat pitched his product, which according to him was easier to inject, easier to handle, and so forth. Medical records filled Lafargue's office, and the walls were "decorated" with photographs showing the results of successful plastic surgery. The Japanese man was waving his arms about as he spoke.

The telephone rang. As Richard listened, a deep frown came over his face, and when he answered his voice was hollow and tremulous. He thanked the caller, then turned to the salesman and explained that he would have to terminate their meeting. They set up another time for the next day.

Lafargue doffed his lab coat and ran all the way to his car. Roger was waiting at the wheel, but he sent him home, preferring to drive himself.

He drove rapidly to the Paris ring road, then took the Normandy turnpike. He kept his foot down and leaned furiously on the horn whenever a driver did not get over into the slow lane quickly enough when he wanted to pass. In under three hours, he reached the psychiatric institution where Viviane was confined.

Once at the château, he leaped from the Mercedes and

bounded up the front steps to the reception window. The receptionist went to find the psychiatrist who was treating Viviane.

Richard followed the doctor into the elevator. When they reached Viviane's door, the psychiatrist nodded toward the plexiglass observation window, and Richard looked in.

Viviane was in crisis. She had ripped her smock, and she was stamping her feet and screaming, tearing at her body, which was already covered with bloody weals.

"How long?" Richard asked in a whisper,

"Since this morning. We've given her injections, tranquilizers. They should take effect soon."

"She can't be left like that! Double the dose. Poor kid..."

His hands were shaking uncontrollably. He braced himself on the door to Viviane's room, pressing his forehead against it and biting his upper lip.

"Viviane, my baby! Viviane! Open the door—I'm going in."

"That's not a very good idea," said the psychiatrist dubiously. "The presence of other people makes her even more agitated."

Exhausted, heaving, crouched in a corner of the room, Viviane was raking her face with her fingernails, and, short as they were, she was drawing blood. Richard came in, sat down on the bed and, his voice no more than a murmur, called her by name. She began screaming again, but she stayed still. She was breathless, and her mad eyes rolled in every direction; she drew back her lips and whistled through her teeth. Little by little, still quite conscious, she settled down. Her breathing was more regular now, less labored. Lafargue was able to take her in his arms and get her into bed. Sitting next to her, he held her hand, stroked her brow, kissed her cheek. The psychiatrist had remained in the doorway, his hands in the pockets of his white coat; he came over to Richard, taking his arm.

"Come on, she should be left alone now."

They went back to the ground floor and took a little walk together outside in the grounds.

"It's just awful," Lafargue mumbled.

"I know. You shouldn't come so often. It doesn't do any good, so why put yourself through it?"

"No! I must! I just have to come!"

The psychiatrist shrugged, mystified by Lafargue's pressing need to witness such a pitiful spectacle.

"Yes, I really must come every time this happens. Promise you'll let me know, all right?"

His voice broke; he was weeping. He shook the doctor's hand and made his way to his car.

Richard drove faster than ever on the return journey to the house in Le Vésinet. The image of Viviane obsessed him. The vision of her battered and sullied body was a waking nightmare that tormented him always. Viviane! It had all started with a long-drawn-out scream audible above the music of the band, then Viviane had appeared with her clothes torn, her thighs streaming with blood, her eyes blank...

Lise had the day off. He could hear the piano up on the second floor. He burst out laughing, ran and pressed his mouth to the intercom and shouted as loud as he could.

"Good evening! Get dressed! You are going to entertain me tonight!"

The speakers in the dressing-room walls started to vibrate. Lafargue had turned the volume up as far as it would go. The racket was intolerable. Eve gasped. This damned sound system was the one perversion of Lafargue's that she had not been able to cope with.

He found her slumped over the piano, her hands clamped to ears still hurting from the onslaught. He had stopped in the doorway, a smile playing about his lips and a glass of scotch in his hand.

She turned and looked at him in horror. She knew the meaning of the crises that made him erupt like this: in the last year Viviane had had three episodes of high agitation and self-mutilation. It was like salt rubbed in Richard's wound, and he could not put up with the pain. His suffering had to be appeased, and Eve existed solely for this purpose.

"Let's go, you piece of trash!"

He held out a glass of scotch, and when she hesitated to take it he grabbed the young woman by the hair and twisted her head back. He forced her to empty the glass in one gulp. Then he seized her wrist, dragged her all the way downstairs, and threw her bodily into the car.

It was eight o'clock when they entered the studio apartment in Rue Godot-de-Mauroy. Lafargue propelled Eve onto the bed by kicking her in the back.

"Get undressed! Fast!"

Eve stripped. He already had the closet open and was pulling out clothes, tossing them pell-mell onto the carpet. She stood facing him, crying softly. He held out the leather skirt, the boots, a white blouse. She put them on. He pointed to the telephone.

"Call Varneroy!"

Eve shuddered, gagging with disgust, but Richard's expression was terrible, almost demonic. She was obliged to pick up the receiver and dial the number.

After a moment, Varneroy came on the line. He

immediately recognized Eve's voice. Richard stood behind her, ready to strike.

"My dear Eve," burbled the caller in a nasal voice, "have you recovered from our last meeting? And you need money? How sweet of you to think of poor old Varneroy!"

Eve made the appointment. Thrilled, Varneroy would be there in half an hour. He was a crank that Eve had "recruited" one night on Boulevard des Capucines at the time when Richard was still forcing her to find customers on the street. She had made enough connections at the time to supply the twice-monthly sessions that he now demanded of her: those who still called the studio apartment gave Richard quite enough choice to assuage his need to debase the young woman.

"Try to rise to the occasion," he sneered. Then he disappeared, slamming the door behind him. She knew that he would be spying on her from the other side of the one-way mirror.

The treatment she got at the hands of Varneroy made it impossible to take him on too frequently. So Eve would call him only after one of Viviane's crises. Varneroy was perfectly willing to accept Eve's hesitancy; and, after urgent appeals from him had been rejected on several occasions, he had resigned himself to leaving a telephone number with Eve where she could reach him whenever she was prepared to submit to his whims.

Varneroy arrived pleased as Punch. He was a pink little man, paunchy, well turned out, and amiable. He took off his hat, laid his jacket down carefully, and kissed Eve on either cheek before opening his bag and producing his whip.

Richard observed these preliminaries with satisfaction, his hands tightly clasped around the armrests of the rocking-chair and his face rife with tics.

Under Varneroy's direction Eve executed a grotesque dance step. The whip cracked. Richard clapped his hands. He laughed uproariously. But then, suddenly overcome by nausea, he could no longer abide the spectacle. The suffering of Eve, who was his, whose destiny he had shaped, whose life he had fashioned, filled him with a mixture of disgust and pity. Varneroy's leering countenance so revolted him that he leaped to his feet and charged into the adjoining apartment.

Stunned by this apparition, Varneroy froze, his jaw slack, his arm aloft. Lafargue snatched the whip from his grasp, grabbed him by the scruff of the neck and ejected him into the hallway. Wide-eyed, mystified, and at a complete loss for words, the weirdo bounded down the stairs without a backward glance.

Richard and Eve were alone. She had fallen to her knees. Richard helped her up, then helped her wash. She got back into the sweatshirt and jeans she had been wearing when she was taken aback by his voice booming through the intercom.

Without a word, he drove her back to the house, undressed her, and laid her on her bed. Considerately, tenderly, he applied ointment to her wounds and made her very hot tea.

He held her to him, bringing the cup to her mouth and letting her take tiny sips. Then he drew the sheet up over her chest and stroked her hair. He had dissolved a sleeping tablet in her tea, and she quickly fell asleep.

Richard left Eve's room, went out into the garden, and made for the pond. The two swans slept side by side, heads beneath their wings, the female, so graceful, nuzzled against the more imposing body of the male.

He admired their serenity, longing for the soothing power of such calm. He wept bitter tears. He had snatched Eve from the hands of Varncroy, and he knew full well that this pity—for that is what he called it—had abruptly destroyed the hate, the limitless, unrestrained hate that was his only reason for living.

Mygale often played chess with you. He would think for a long time before risking a move that you never anticipated. Sometimes he improvised attacks without regard for his own defenses; he was impulsive, yet invincible.

The day came when he did away with your shackles and replaced your mat with a sofa. On this you slept and lolled all day long amid silky cushions. Meanwhile, the heavy door to the cellar remained firmly padlocked.

Mygale gave you candy and Virginia cigarettes. He inquired about your tastes in music. Your conversations took on a playful cast bordering on small talk. He had provided a videocassette player and brought movies for the two of you to watch together. He made tea, plied you with herbal decoctions, and, if you seemed depressed, he would uncork a bottle of champagne. No sooner were your glasses empty than he would refill them.

You were no longer naked: Mygale had given you an embroidered shawl, a gorgeous piece of fabric beautifully wrapped. With your delicate fingers you had pulled off the paper to reveal the shawl; this gift gave you the greatest pleasure.

Swathed in the shawl, you would snuggle among the cushions, smoking the imported cigarettes or sucking on sugary bonbons, and await your daily visit from Mygale, who would never arrive empty-handed.

His generosity toward you was seemingly boundless. One day the door to the cellar opened and he entered, pushing an enormous object on wheels before him, not without difficulty.

He smiled as he contemplated the tissue paper that enveloped it, the pink ribbon, the bouquet of flowers on the top...

As you stared in amazement, he reminded you of the date: the twenty-second of July. Yes, you had been a captive for ten months, and today you were twenty-one. You hammed it up then, prancing around the giant package, clapping your hands and laughing. Mygale helped you untie the ribbon. You already knew from the shape that it was a piano—but not that it was a Steinway!

Seated on your old stool, once you had loosened up your unwilling fingers, you played. The performance was hardly brilliant, but you shed tears of joy.

And you—you, Vincent Moreau, this monster's pet, his lapdog, his monkey or parrot, whom he had so thoroughly broken—yes, you, had then kissed his hand, giggling with glee.

That was when he slapped you for the second time.

Alex was fretting in his hideout. Surfeited with sleep, his eyes puffy, he spent most of his waking hours in front of the tube. He chose not to think about his future and strove to occupy himself as best he could. In contrast to his custom at the farmhouse, he cleaned house and washed dishes with extreme fastidiousness. Everything was sparkling clean, and he would pass hours at a time polishing the floor or scouring pots and pans.

His thigh no longer hurt much. The forming scar tissue itched a little, but the wound was not painful. A simple compress had replaced the heavy-duty bandage.

One evening some ten days after Alex had set up house, he had a brilliant idea, or at least he convinced himself that it was a brilliant idea. He was watching a soccer match on the box. Sports had never held much interest for him, except for karate. The only periodicals he read in the normal way were martial arts magazines. Still, his eye idly followed the zigzagging of the round ball as it was systematically knocked around by the players. He sipped the last of a glass of wine and began to nod off, not getting up to turn off the set when the game ended. The next show was a "medical special" on plastic surgery.

A commentator presented a report on lifts and other facial reconstruction. Then came an interview with the head of a hospital clinic in Paris, Professor Lafargue. Alex was awake now, and riveted.

"The second stage," Lafargue was saying, using a sketch as a visual aid, "consists in the scraping of the periosteum with what is called a raspatory. This is a very important phase. As you see here, the purpose is to let the periosteum adhere to the deepest layer of the skin so as to cushion it…"

On the screen appeared a series of photographs of faces transformed, remodeled, sculpted, beautified. The patients shown earlier were unrecognizable. Alex had followed the explanation attentively, irritated that he did not understand some of the terms used. When the end credits rolled, he took down the name of the doctor, Lafargue, and the name of the clinic where he worked.

Alex thought about the photograph on his identity card, about the mercenary hospitality of his friend the legionnaire, about the money hidden in the attic of his new abode… Slowly but surely, everything was coming together!

The guy on the tube had claimed that a nose job was a perfectly benign operation, just like the excision of fatty tissues on certain parts of the face. A wrinkle? No problem: the scalpel could wipe it away like an eraser.

Alex rushed to the bathroom and looked at himself in the mirror. He fingered his face, the lump on his nose, the cheeks that were too chubby, the double chin…

It was a cinch! The doctor had said two weeks—just two weeks to redesign a face! You simply wipe away the old one and replace it with a new. But no, nothing was ever that simple. He would have to convince the surgeon to work on him—and Alex was a criminal wanted by the police. How could he find a lever powerful enough to make the man keep quiet—to make him carry through the operation successfully and then let him go without tipping off the authorities? Did this Lafargue perhaps have kids or a wife?

Alex read and re-read what he had written down on a piece of paper: the name of the doctor and the particulars of the hospital where he worked. The more he thought about his idea, the more brilliant it seemed. His dependence on the legionnaire would significantly diminish once his appearance was altered, for the police would then be looking for a phantom, an Alex Barny that didn't exist, and getting out of the country would be far easier to arrange.

He did not sleep a wink that night. The next day he got up at the crack of dawn, washed rapidly, trimmed his own hair, and meticulously ironed the suit and shirt that he had brought from the farmhouse. The Citroën was waiting in the garage...

Mygale was a delight. His visits grew longer. He brought you the newspapers, and he often took his meals with you. The cellar was insufferably hot—it was August—but he had installed a refrigerator, which he restocked every day with fruit juice. In addition to the shawl, your wardrobe now included a light dressing gown and a pair of mules.

In the fall, Mygale began giving you the injections. He came down to see you, syringe in hand. At his direction, you lay down on the sofa and bared your buttocks. The needle popped promptly into your flesh. You had seen the translucent pink-tinged liquid in the barrel of the syringe, and now it was inside you.

Mygale was very gentle and tried hard not to hurt you, but the liquid itself caused you pain once it was injected. Then, as it dispersed in your body, the pain wore off.

You did not question Mygale about this treatment. You were completely taken up by your drawing and your piano; the intense creative activity sated you. What did it matter about the shots? Mygale was so sweet.

You were making rapid strides with your music. Mygale rummaged devotedly for hours in music shops for scores. Manuals on painting and art books showing exemplary works were piling up in the cellar.

One day you let slip the sinister nickname you had given him. It was at the end of a meal eaten together. The champagne had gone to your head. Blushing, stuttering, you had admitted your error—uttering the words "my fault"—and he had smiled indulgently.

The injections continued, regular as clockwork. But they were no more than a mildly disagreeable interruption in your life of leisure.

For your twenty-second birthday Mygale moved more furniture into the cellar. The spotlight was replaced by soft-light lamps with shades. The sofa was joined by armchairs, a low table, and poufs. A thick carpet was laid across the floor.

Quite some time earlier, Mygale had set up a folding shower stall in a corner of the cellar. A field washstand completed these arrangements, along with a commode. Mygale even thought to curtain off this toilet area out of consideration for your modesty.

You tried on the bathrobe and pulled a face at the color of the bath towels. These Mygale then changed.

Cooped up in the confines of the cellar, you dreamed of space, of wind. You painted trompe-l'oeil windows on the walls. On one side a mountain landscape had appeared, flooded with sunlight and the sparkling white of eternal snows. A halogen lamp directed at the peaks shed a blinding clarity over this artificial outlet onto the outside world. On the other side of your cell, you had covered the cement with a blue rough-cast representation of foaming waves. Deep in the background were the orange-red hues of a magnificent flaming sunset that was your pride and joy.

In addition to the shots, Mygale had you swallow a host of other drugs: multicolored capsules, tasteless lozenges, vials of liquid to be diluted in water…The labels had always been removed from the packaging. Mygale wanted to know whether this worried you. You shrugged and replied that you trusted him. Mygale stroked your cheek. At this you grasped his hand and placed a kiss in the middle of his palm. Mygale flinched, and just for a moment you thought he was going to hit you again, but then his expression softened, and he left his hand in yours. You turned away so that he would not see the tears of joy welling at the corners of your eyes.

You had grown pale from living so long out of the daylight. But then Mygale brought in a bench and a sunlamp, and you began sunbathing. You were delighted to see your body getting so beautifully brown, and you soon showed off a spectacular all-over tan to your friend; how happy you were when he intimated that he shared your satisfaction with this transformation!

Days, weeks, months went by, seemingly monotonous, yet

actually enriched for you by many and intense pleasures; the joy you felt at the piano or the easel was profoundly fulfilling.

You had lost every trace of sexual desire. With considerable embarrassment you had asked Mygale about this. He acknowledged that your food contained substances intended to have this effect. It was simply, said Mygale, so that you would not be tormented, considering that you never saw anyone but him. You said yes, you quite understood. And he promised you that soon, when you started going out, and when the additives were removed from your diet, you would once again feel desire.

In the night, alone in your cellar, you would sometimes vainly rub your limp penis; but the bitterness you felt dissipated at the thought that you were soon going to "go out." Mygale had promised you, so you didn't have to worry...

4

Alex drove cautiously to Paris, taking great care not to break any traffic rules. He had even thought of taking the bus and the metro, but he had rejected this idea for one good reason: Lafargue would surely have a car, and he would not be able to tail him.

He parked opposite the hospital entrance. It was very early. Alex was well aware that the doctor was unlikely to report to his office at the break of dawn, but he needed to inspect the area ahead of time, to get a feel for the place. On a wall alongside the gates was a large board listing the specialized services offered by the hospital and naming the physicians in charge of each. Sure enough, Lafargue's name was clearly displayed.

Alex strolled up and down the street, holding tightly onto the butt of the dead cop's Colt in his jacket pocket. After a while he went and sat at a café terrace with a good view of the hospital's staff entrance.

Finally, about ten o'clock, a car stopped at the traffic light a few yards from where Alex was stationed: a red Mercedes driven by a chauffeur. Alex immediately recognized Lafargue, who was sitting in the back reading a newspaper.

The Mercedes waited for the light to change, then took the drive that led to the hospital's parking lot. Alex saw Lafargue get out. The chauffeur stayed in the car for a while, but it was a very hot day, and before long he made his way over to the café and, like Alex, sat on the terrace.

Roger ordered a draft beer. His boss had an important operation scheduled, but would be leaving right after for a meeting at his private clinic in Boulogne.

The license plate of Lafargue's car bore the number 78, designating the department of Yvelines. Alex knew the number of every French department by heart; during his lonely sojourn in the farmhouse he had broken the monotony by memorizing them, reciting the list in numerical order, and setting himself posers: if he read in the newspaper that an eighty-year-old man had remarried, he would say to himself, "Eighty? That's the department of the Somme."

The chauffeur did not seem to be in any hurry. With his elbows on the café table, he was doing a crossword, his attention completely focused on the grid of the puzzle. Alex paid his check and went into a post office next door to the hospital. He could no longer keep an eye on the hospital gate, but it would be strikingly bad luck, he thought, if the doc were to up and leave in the next fifteen minutes or so.

He thumbed through a phone book in search of Lafargues. Lafargue is a common name, and there were pages of them. But not so many without an "s" on the end and with just one "f." And Lafargues who were doctors were, of course, even rarer. In department 78 there were just three. One lived in Saint-Germain, another at Plaisir, and the third in Le Vésinet. The right Dr. Lafargue had to be one of them. Alex noted down all three addresses.

Back at the café, he made sure that the chauffeur was still there. When noon approached, the waiter started setting up the tables for lunch. He appeared to know the chauffeur well, because he asked him if he would be eating lunch today.

Roger replied in the negative: the boss had to get to Boulogne as soon as possible, and they would leave the moment he got out of the operating room.

Sure enough, the surgeon soon appeared. He got into the Mercedes, and the chauffeur slid behind the wheel. Alex followed their car. They left the center of Paris and made for Boulogne. Tailing them was not difficult, for Alex knew where they were headed.

Roger parked in front of a private clinic and was soon back to his crossword. Mistrustful of his memory, Alex wrote down the name of the street on a piece of paper. It was a long wait. He paced up and down at a nearby intersection, trying not to draw attention to himself. Then he sat down in a little park and went on waiting without ever taking his eye off the Mercedes. He had left his own car door unlocked so he could start up as quickly as possible should the doctor suddenly appear.

The surgery planning meeting lasted just over an hour. Richard barely unclenched his teeth the whole time. He was sickly pale and hollow-cheeked. Since Eve's session with Varneroy, he had been on automatic pilot.

Alex had gone into a café for a fresh supply of cigarettes when Roger, spotting Lafargue in the clinic lobby, got out and opened the rear door of the Mercedes. Alex returned to the Citroën CX and followed once more, hanging back a good distance. Once he perceived that they were clearly headed for Le Vésinet, he peeled off. There was no point in risking being spotted when he had Lafargue's address in his pocket.

He went over there later on. Lafargue's place was impressive, though the bounding wall hindered any clear view of its façade. Alex inspected the neighboring houses. The street was deserted. It was not a good idea to stay too long. He noticed how many windows were shuttered. Le Vésinet had been abandoned for August. It was four o'clock, and Alex hesitated. He intended to investigate the surgeon's house that same night, but didn't know what to do in the meantime. For lack of a better plan, he decided to talk a walk in the forest of Saint-Germain, which was very close.

He returned to Le Vésinet around nine and parked the CX a good way away from Lafargue's street. Night was beginning to fall, but you could still see. He climbed a wall surrounding a nearby house to get a look into Lafargue's grounds. Sitting astride the top of the wall, he was pretty well camouflaged by the dense foliage of an abundantly spreading chestnut tree. From far off he was invisible, and if anyone should happen to come walking down the street he could retreat even farther in among the branches.

He took in the lawn, the pond, the trees, the swimming pool. Lafargue was dining al fresco, in company with a woman. Alex smiled. This was a good beginning. Were there perhaps children? Not likely, for they would be eating with their parents. They could be away on vacation, of course. Or they might be toddlers and already in bed. But Lafargue was about fifty, so his children, if he had any, should at least be adolescents. There was no chance of them being in bed at ten o'clock on a summer evening. What was more, no lights could be seen in the house, either on the ground floor or upstairs. A garden lamp gave off a rather feeble light in the vicinity of the table at which the couple were sitting.

Satisfied, Alex got off his perch and dropped to the sidewalk. He grimaced, for his still tender thigh could not yet take such shocks. He returned to the CX to wait for full darkness. He was nervous, and he began chain-smoking. At ten-thirty, he made his way back to the Lafargue place. The street was as empty as before. A car horn hooted in the distance.

He followed the bounding wall along till, at the end of the property, he came upon a large wooden crate containing spades, rakes, and other tools belonging to the municipal roadworkers. He climbed up on it, hauled himself onto the top of the wall, got his balance, and, judging the distance, jumped down into the grounds. Crouching in a clump of trees, he waited; if there was a dog, it wouldn't take long to make its presence felt. No bark came. Alex appraised the shrubs near him, then proceeded along the wall. He was looking for reliable footholds susceptible of helping him back up over the wall on his way out. Near the pond was a mock grotto made of concrete that served as nighttime shelter for the swans. It was built up against the wall and was three or four feet tall. Alex smiled and checked it out: it would be child's play to go this way over the wall back into the street outside. Reassured, he went farther into the grounds, passing the swimming pool. Lafargue and his companion had gone inside, and the immediate surroundings of the house were deserted. Strips of light filtered through closed shutters on the second floor.

Soft music came from the windows. A piano. It was not a recording, because the playing kept stopping and going back. On the other end of the house were more lighted windows. Alex melted into the wall, seeking to disappear in the ivy that covered the front of the building. Lafargue was leaning on one of the balustrades on the second floor, looking at the sky. Alex held his breath. Several minutes passed like this, until the doctor at last closed the window.

❖

Alex dithered for a long time: should he chance entering the house or not? Yes, he decided, because he needed to reconnoiter, at least a little, so as to know where he was treading when he came back to kidnap the surgeon's wife.

The house was large, and light was coming from every upstairs window. Lafargue must sleep in a separate room from his wife. That did not surprise Alex: everyone knew that bourgeois married couples don't always sleep in the same bed!

Clutching the Colt, he climbed the steps and turned the front-door knob. There was no resistance; very gently, he pushed the door inward.

He took one step. There was a large room to his left and another to his right; before him was a staircase. The woman's bedroom was upstairs to the right.

A bourgeois woman like her didn't get up early. The bitch would lie in bed every morning. All Alex would have to do was watch for Lafargue to leave and then run up and take her by surprise while she was still asleep.

He closed the door silently behind him, darted just as silently across the grass, scrambled up onto the grotto, and tumbled over the wall. It was perfect. But no! There was a hitch. Okay, the lackey of a chauffeur would leave with his boss. But what if there was a maid? It would be a disaster if he ran into some old biddy there to do the housework!

Alex reached the Paris ring road, still taking care to obey all the rules of the road. It was midnight by the time he got back to his little house in Livry-Gargan.

Early the next morning, he returned to Le Vésinet. On tenterhooks, he watched Lafargue's house, quite convinced an extra domestic would soon arrive. He had to snatch

Lafargue's wife without witnesses. The surgeon would then surely capitulate when confronted by the choice: give me a new face or I'll kill your wife. But if someone happened to see the abduction, a domestic of one sort or another, a gardener, anybody at all, they would immediately call the cops, and Alex's great scheme would be a dead letter.

Alex was lucky. Lafargue did employ a maid. But Lise had gone on vacation two days earlier. Of the five weeks the doctor allowed her in the year, she took three in the summer, when she went to her sister's in the Morvan, and the rest during the winter.

So the whole morning went by, and still no one had shown up at the Lafargue place. Somewhat reassured, Alex raced back to Paris. It occurred to him that perhaps Lafargue did not go to work every day. If he took a day off during the week, Alex needed to know it right away. He decided he could ask the people in Lafargue's office at the hospital about this; it would be easy to make up some rigmarole.

The chauffeur was waiting for his boss, as he did every day, on the café terrace across the street from the hospital. Alex, who was dying of thirst, had ordered a draft beer at the bar. As he brought it eagerly to his lips, he saw Roger leap to his feet. Lafargue was standing in the parking lot hailing his driver. The two men conferred briefly, then Roger gave the car keys to the surgeon and walked off muttering to himself in the direction of the nearby metro station. Alex was already at the wheel of his Citroën CX.

Lafargue drove like a man possessed. He did not head toward Boulogne. Alex, in great alarm, saw him veer off toward the ring road and the highway.

The prospect of a long-distance tail did not thrill Alex in the least. Without taking his eyes off Lafargue's car, he mulled things over...Lafargue has kids, he thought. That was it: they must be on vacation, and he has just received some kind of bad news. Maybe one of them has been taken ill, and he has to go and see them? Otherwise, why should he have left work earlier than usual and sent his flunky home? Could the bastard have a mistress? Yes, more than likely. But would he just suddenly go off and see her in the middle of the day? This was crazy!

Lafargue continued at top speed, weaving between the other cars. Alex kept up with him, sweating with fear at the thought of a spot check by the national security police at a toll booth. But before long the Mercedes was off the turnpike and barreling along a winding country road without significantly slowing down. Alex was almost ready to give up the chase, feeling sure he was about to be spotted. But Lafargue did not so much as glance in his rearview mirror. Viviane was having another of her crises, and, true to his word, the psychiatrist had telephoned. Richard was fully aware of how this visit to his daughter—the second in a single week—was going to affect him. He also knew that this evening, back at Le Vésinet, he would not ask Eve to call Varneroy. After what had happened the last time, that was now impossible. But how, then, was he going to find consolation?

The Mercedes pulled up at the entrance to a château. A discreet sign indicated that it was a mental home. Alex scratched his head in perplexity.

Richard went straight up to Viviane's room without waiting for the doctor. There the same sight as before awaited him: his daughter in a state of wild agitation, stamping her feet, trying to injure herself. He did not enter the room, but remained with his face pressed against the observation window, sobbing quietly. The psychiatrist, who had been informed of his arrival, came up to find him, then helped him back down to the ground floor, where the two men went into an office for privacy.

"I'll not come back here again. It's too hard. I just can't bear it, you understand."

"I understand perfectly."

"Does she need anything? Bedclothes? Anything at all?"

"What could she possibly need? You must pull yourself together, Dr. Lafargue. Your daughter is never going to get out of this. Please don't think me insensitive. You have to face facts. She is going to remain in a vegetative state, interrupted from time to time by crises of the type you have just witnessed. We can give her tranquilizers, knock her out with neuroleptics. But basically we have no serious options, as you well know. Psychiatry is not like surgery. We can't change appearances. We don't have the precision 'therapeutic' tools that you people have."

Richard was calming down, recovering his poise little by little and reassuming a distant attitude.

"Yes, yes, I'm sure you're right."

"I would like—I want to get your agreement—please give me permission not to telephone you every time Viviane—"

"I agree. Don't call anymore."

Richard rose, took his leave of the psychiatrist, and returned to his car. Alex watched him emerge from the château. But this time he didn't start his own car. The odds were overwhelming that Lafargue was on his way back to his house in Le Vésinet, or to Boulogne, or to the hospital.

Alex went to get lunch in the village. The square was clogged—a traveling fair was setting up its rides. He wondered who it could be living in that rathole with all the crazy people. If it was a kid of Lafargue's, he must love him a lot to quit work like that and race off to see him.

Filled with a sudden resolve, Alex pushed away a plate still half-covered with greasy fries and asked for his check. He went and bought a large bouquet of flowers and a box of candy, and headed back to the nuthouse.

The receptionist greeted him in the entrance hall.

"Are you here to visit a patient?"

"Hmm, yes."

"What name, please?"

"Lafargue."

"Lafargue!"

The receptionist seemed so amazed that Alex felt sure he had blundered. He began to think that Lafargue must have a psychiatric nurse for a lover.

"But...you have never been here before to see Viviane, have you?"

"No, it's the first time. I'm her cousin."

The receptionist studied Alex in surprise for a moment, hesitating.

"You won't be able to see Viviane today. She isn't well. Didn't Dr. Lafargue tell you?"

"No. I was supposed to—my visit was planned a while ago, you see..."

"I really don't understand this. Viviane's father was here less than an hour ago."

"He had no way of reaching me: I've been on the road since this morning."

The receptionist nodded and shrugged her shoulders. She took the flowers and candy and put them on her desk.

"I'll give her all these later. Today there's really no point. Follow me, please."

They took the elevator. Alex padded behind the woman,

his arms dangling. At the door to Viviane's room, the receptionist motioned Alex to look through the observation window. He started at the sight of Viviane crumpled in one corner of the room, staring maliciously at the door.

"I can't let you go in today. I hope you understand."

Alex understood. His palms were moist, and he felt nauseous. He kept on looking at the madwoman: he had the feeling he had seen her somewhere before. But that was obviously impossible.

He left the asylum as quickly as he could. Even if Lafargue simply adored this madwoman, Alex could never kidnap her. He might just as well turn himself in to the cops right away! In any case, how could he pull it off? He would have to take the château by siege! How would he even get into her cell? No, it was Lafargue's wife who would have to be the hostage.

He drove carefully back to the Paris area, and it was already late by the time he reached his hideaway at Livry-Gargan.

The next morning, he resumed his vigil outside the Lafargue place. He was tense, anxious—but not really afraid. All night long he had mulled over his plan, imagining the results of the transformation of his face.

Roger arrived at eight o'clock, alone, on foot, his sports paper tucked under his arm. Alex was parked some fifty yards from the front gate. He knew he would have to wait some more; Lafargue usually aimed to get to the hospital by ten.

About nine-thirty, the Mercedes pulled up to the gate. Roger got out to open it, drove through, then stopped once more to slam it shut. Alex sighed with relief to see Lafargue leaving.

The ideal thing would be to take the bitch by surprise while she was still asleep. There was no time to lose. Alex had seen no other household help over the last few days, but you could never be sure. He started the car and drew up just opposite the Lafargue place. Turning the handle of the gate, he strode through as naturally as you please and set off across the grounds.

He approached the house with one hand in his pocket clasping the butt of the Colt. The shutters of the upstairs rooms on the right were closed, and Alex was surprised to notice for the first time that they were fastened from the outside, as though the windows had been closed up permanently. He was sure, all the same, that he had seen lights on and heard a piano playing behind those shutters.

Alex shrugged and continued reconnoitering. Before long, he had circled the whole place and found himself at the foot of the front steps. He drew a deep breath before opening the front door. The ground floor was just as he had glimpsed it the night before: the large drawing room, the library-office and, between them, the staircase to the next floor. He climbed the stairs, his breath bated and the Colt now out of his pocket.

Someone was humming on the far side of a bolted door—bolted, indeed, three times over. Incredulous, Alex's first thought was that the surgeon must be mad: why would he lock his wife up like this? But then perhaps she really was a piece of work. Perhaps he was right not to trust her. Ever so carefully, Alex slid back the top bolt. The woman was still humming to herself. The second bolt. Then the third. What if the door was locked with a key, too? His heart beat faster as he turned the knob of the last bolt. But the door slowly opened, with no squeaking of hinges.

The bitch was sitting at a dressing table making herself up. Alex pressed himself against the wall so as not to appear in her mirror. Her back was to him; she was absorbed in her makeup. She was beautiful, her waist was narrow, her buttocks—squashed onto the stool—were muscular. Alex leaned down and laid his Colt on the carpet, then he was upon her, his fist coming down sharply on the exposed nape of her neck.

The blow was an expert one, carefully gauged. In Meaux, at the nightclub where he had worked as a bouncer, mayhem had been frequent. He had learned how to deal swiftly with troublemakers—how to deliver such a sharp blow to the skull that layabouts needed only dragging out and dumping on the sidewalk.

The woman lay inert on the carpet. Alex was trembling. He felt her pulse and got an urge to caress her, but it was hardly the moment for that. He went back downstairs. At the bar he found scotch, grabbed the bottle, and took a long swig.

Leaving the house, he opened the front gates wide and, restraining an impulse to run, went to the Citroën CX and started it up. He drove into the grounds and pulled up at the house, just at the foot of the front steps. Then he ran up to the bedroom. She was still motionless. He bound her carefully with cord brought from the trunk of the CX and gagged her with adhesive tape. Then he wrapped her in a bedspread.

Taking her in his arms, he carried her downstairs and closed her in the trunk. Once more he drank from the whisky bottle, emptying it and tossing it onto the ground. He climbed into the driver's seat and started the car. Out on the road, an elderly couple were walking a dog, but they paid no attention to Alex.

He made for Paris, crossing the city from west to east on

his way back to Livry-Gargan. He stared into the rearview mirror, but no one was following.

Back at his house, he opened the trunk and carried Madame Lafargue, still wrapped in the bedspread, down to the cellar. To be doubly sure, he tied the cord to a motorcycle antitheft device, a thick chain covered in plastic. This he padlocked to a radiator pipe.

He put out the light and left the cellar, returning a little later with a saucepan full of cold water, which he threw over the young woman's head. She began to wriggle, but her movements were restricted by the cord. She moaned, being unable to cry out. Alex grinned in the darkness. She had never seen his face and would not be able to describe him when he let her go. If he ever let her go...The surgeon, though, would see him, see his face. He might even make an Identi-Kit picture of him once the operation was done. Lafargue would be able to describe Alex's new face. The face of the self-same Alex who had killed a cop—and kidnapped Lafargue's own wife! Never mind, thought Alex, the main thing for now is to get this guy to operate on me.

The rest could wait till later. Later, he would certainly have to kill Lafargue and his wife.

He went back up to his bedroom, delighted with the success of the first part of his plan. He would wait till evening, for Lafargue's return to Le Vésinet, and his shock at finding the bitch gone; then he would pay a call on the surgeon and tell him what the deal was. This was hardball! They were all going to see, all those shits, just what sort of stuff Alex was made of!

He poured himself a glass of wine, smacking his lips after drinking. As for that bitch, he was going to do her in more ways than one. Why not? Business should be mixed with pleasure.

But take it slow. First, take care of Lafargue. He could see about the sex stuff later.

III

The Prey

1

This is horrible! It is all starting again. You don't understand it—or, rather, you are afraid you understand it all too well. This time, Mygale is going to kill you!

For three days he didn't say a word to you. He brought your meals up to your room, but wouldn't even look at you. When he had burst into the studio apartment and put an end to the whipping from the crazed Varneroy, you had been dumbfounded. He was cracking, obviously: never before had he let pity show. Back at Le Vésinet, he had been tender, attentive to your pain. He had put ointment on your wounds, and in amazement you had seen his eyes brimming with tears.

This morning you had heard him leave for the hospital. Then he had come back, leaped at you, and knocked you down. And here you are, a prisoner once more, back in the cellar chained up in the dark.

Hell is about to return, just like four years ago, after he caught you in the forest.

He is going to kill you. Mygale has gone mad, far madder than before. Viviane has had another crisis. He has been to see her in Normandy, and he can't stand it. Pimping you no longer works. What will he think up?

He had changed so much over these last few months. He was far less mean. True, he would still scream into his damned intercom to shake you up, but...

Just as well to die, anyway. You never had the courage to

kill yourself. He has eradicated every vestige of revolt in you. Vincent has become his creature. Eve has become his creature. You are nothing, nothing at all.

You used to dream often of escape. But where would you go, the state you were in? Back to your mother, your friends? Alex? Who would even recognize you? Mygale has succeeded: he has bound you to him forever.

You hope that the end will be quick. Let him finish you off, but stop toying with you!

Mygale has tied the rope solidly, and you can't move. The thing irritates your breasts and binds them tight. They hurt.

Your breasts…

Yes, your breasts. He had worked so hard getting them to sprout. It was not long after the first injections that they had begun to grow. You paid no attention at first, attributing the appearance of masses of fatty tissue to the indolent life you were leading. But at each of his visits Mygale would palpate your chest and nod. The implication was unavoidable. Horrified, you watched your chest swelling, your breasts taking form. Day after day you gauged the growth of your mammaries and clutched your despairingly flaccid penis. You wept over this often. Mygale would reassure you. Everything was going fine. Did you need anything? What could he get you that you did not already have? He was just so nice, so considerate.

After a time, you stopped weeping. To forget, you painted or spent long hours at the piano. Nothing changed. Mygale visited you more and more frequently. It was ridiculous. You had known each other for two years; he had destroyed all shame in you: at the beginning of your imprisonment, you used to relieve yourself in front of him. But now, you would hide your breasts from him. You were continually pulling your dressing gown closed in front. Mygale had had you try on a bra. It served no good purpose, because your tits were hard and firm. But you felt better with it: in bra and blouse you were far more at ease.

As earlier with the chains, the cellar, or the injections, you gradually got used to your new body; in the end, it felt perfectly familiar. And, after all, what good did thinking do?

There was your hair, too. In the early days, Mygale used to cut it. Then he let it grow. Whether or not because of the shots, the capsules, and the vials, it became fluffier. Mygale gave you shampoos, even a blow-dryer. You took pleasure in taking care of it. You tried various styles, a chignon, a ponytail, then you adopted curls and stuck with them.

He is going to kill you. It is hot in the cellar; the old thirst is coming back. Not long ago, he hosed you down with icy water, but you weren't allowed to drink.

You are waiting for death. Nothing matters anymore. You remember high school, the village, the girls—yes, the girls. And your pal Alex. You will never see any of them again; you will never see anything again. You had grown used to solitude; your only company was Mygale. At times you felt waves of nostalgia, attacks of depression. He gave you tranquilizers, swamped you with presents…The bastard! All that, and you end up like this!

What is he waiting for? Is he devising refinements of cruelty, planning the mise-en-scène of your demise? Will he kill you with his own hands or hand you over to some Varneroy?

No! The fact is he can no longer stand anyone else touching you, even approaching you. You could see that by the way he struck that nutty Varneroy. He had really been hurting you with his whip.

Could it be your own fault? You had been mocking him recently. No sooner did he enter your room, if you were at the piano, than you would play him "The Man I Love," a tune you knew he loathed. Or else—and this was more perverse—you would be outrageously provocative. He has lived alone for many years. Did he once have a mistress? No—he is incapable of love.

You noticed how uncomfortable he was when he saw you naked. You were certain he wanted you, but was repelled by the idea of touching you—which was, of course, understandable enough. Still, he desired you. You were always walking around naked in your room. Once, you pivoted round to face him on your piano stool, spread your thighs, and opened your vulva in front of him. You saw his Adam's apple shift; you saw him redden. That was what made him even more furious: to want you, after everything he had done to you; to want you, despite what you were!

How long is he going to let you rot in this cellar? The first time, after the chase in the forest, he had left you for eight days there in the darkness. Eight days! He had admitted it to you later.

If only you had not toyed with his desires, perhaps he would not be taking his revenge on you like this now?

And yet, it is silly to think about it like that: the problem is Viviane—Viviane, crazy as a cuckoo for the last four years. The more the time goes by, the more obvious it is that she is incurable. And he just can't accept that. He just can't admit that that wreck is his own daughter. How old is she now? She was sixteen, so now she's twenty. And you? You were twenty, and now you're twenty-four...

It's not fair, to die at twenty-four. Die? You've been dead for two years already! Vincent died two years ago. What does it matter about the ghost he left behind?

Just a ghost—but a ghost that can still feel pain, infinite pain. True, you don't want him to go on pawing you, and pawing is the word—you have had a bellyful of his tricks, his sick manipulations. But now you are going to suffer more—God knows what he is capable of thinking up. He is an expert when it comes to torture; he has already proved that to you.

You are trembling. You want to smoke. You miss the opium: yesterday he gave you some, and you took it. That moment, always in the evening, when he comes to see you and fills the pipe for you, is one of your greatest delights. The first time, you were nauseated, you threw up. But he persisted. It was the day you could no longer deny the evidence of your eyes: your breasts were getting larger! He caught you by surprise in your cellar, weeping. To console you, he offered you a new record. But you showed him your breasts: your throat was tight; you could not utter a word. He left and came back a few minutes later with the necessaries: the pipe and the greasy little balls. A poisoned gift. Mygale is a spider with more poisons than one. You let yourself be talked into it, and thereafter it was you who asked for the drug if he ever forgot the daily ritual. The disgust for opium you felt in the first days is long gone. One day, after smoking, you fell asleep in his arms. You exhaled the last puffs from the pipe; he sat close up against you on the sofa. Mechanically, he caressed your cheek, stroking the smooth skin. Unwittingly, you had helped him transform you, for your beard had never developed. As kids, you and Alex had watched eagerly for the first whiskers to appear, the first down on the upper lip. It was not long before Alex had grown a moustache, sparse at first but soon quite thick. As for you, not a hair manifested itself. For Mygale, this was simply one less thing to worry about. Of course—and he told you this himself—it wouldn't have made any difference: the estrogen injections would have made you smooth-cheeked, anyway. Still, you hated yourself for corresponding so well to his intent, with your beautiful girlish face, as Alex used to say once upon a time…

As for your delicate, finely jointed body, it had driven Mygale wild. He had asked you, one evening, if you were homosexual too. You did not understand this "too." No, you were not queer. The temptation might have entered your mind now and then, but no, there had never really been anything like that. And

Mygale was not that way, as you had suspected at first. You thought of the time he had approached you, to feel you. You had mistaken his examination for a caress. You were still chained up, remember, it was right at the beginning. Timidly, you had reached out to touch him. And he had struck you!

You had been shattered. Why was he holding you captive if not to put you to use as a sexual plaything? That was the only explanation you had been able to find for the treatment he had meted out to you. He had to be a vile homosexual maniac in need of a tame boy-toy. This thought filled you with rage at first, but then you told yourself: to hell with it, I'll play the game, let him do what he wants to me. But one day I'll get away, and I'll come back with Alex, and we'll blow his head off!

But it was a different game you ended up playing, drawn in gradually, unknowingly. A board game whose rules were set by Mygale: a game of snakes and ladders you were bound to lose. One square for torture, another for a gift; one square for injections, another for the piano. One square for Vincent—another for Eve!

Lafargue had had an exhausting afternoon, operating for hours on a child with a badly burned face. The skin of the neck had retracted, obliging him to perform a laborious series of small grafts.

He dismissed Roger upon leaving the hospital and returned alone to Le Vésinet, stopping on the way at a florist and having him put together a magnificent bouquet.

When he saw the door to Eve's upstairs rooms unbolted and wide open, he dropped his flowers and flew up the stairs in great alarm. The piano stool had been knocked over and a vase broken. A dress and underclothes were strewn across the floor. The bedspread was nowhere to be seen. A pair of high-heeled shoes, one half-mangled, lay forlornly by the bed.

Richard recalled his mild surprise at discovering the gate to the property open, though Roger had closed it behind them that morning. Could a delivery person have left it like that? Lise would certainly have placed some orders before leaving on her vacation. But what of Eve's disappearance? Had she run off? Had she talked some delivery man, when he found himself in an empty house, into unbolting her door?

Richard cast about vainly for answers, his panic mounting. Why had she never put on the clothes she had obviously laid out in readiness on the bed? Why was the bedspread missing? No, the delivery-man hypothesis was clearly nonsense. Admittedly, something of the sort had happened a year earlier—and it had happened, indeed, while Lise was off. By chance, Richard had got home just in time to overhear Eve, from behind her barred door, begging a delivery man to open it for her. He had been able to reassure the man that everything was as it should be, that his wife was severely depressed, hence the bolts on the door.

Whatever doubts Roger and Lise might have formed had likewise been dispelled by the invoking of Eve's supposed "mental illness." Besides, Richard was affectionate toward the young woman, and over the last year had allowed her out more and more often. On occasion, she even took dinner downstairs. The madwoman spent her days playing the piano and painting, and Lise did the housework in her rooms without thinking twice about it. In fact, everything seemed normal. Eve was continually showered with gifts. One day, Lise had lifted the white cloth covering Eve's easel, and the sight of Richard portrayed as a transvestite sitting at the bar of a night club merely strengthened her belief that all was decidedly not quite right with her mistress's head. Monsieur Lafargue was more than decent to put up with her the way he did. Most people would have had her put away. Of course, it wouldn't look so good, would it, for a big noise like Professor Lafargue to have a wife in the loony bin. Especially when his daughter was already there...

Richard let himself fall back onto the bed. Clutching Eve's dress, he shook his head in desperation.

The telephone rang. He dashed downstairs and grabbed the receiver.

"Lafargue?" The voice was unfamiliar. "I've got your wife."

"How much do you want? Tell me right now. I'll pay it." Lafargue was shouting, but his voice cracked.

"Take it easy. That's not it. I don't give a shit about money. At least, we'll see if you can give me some money, too."

"For God's sake, tell me! Is she alive?"

"Of course she is."

"Don't you hurt her!"

"Don't worry. I won't mess her up."

"Well, then?"

"I have to see you. Have a little chat."

Alex told Lafargue to meet him at ten o'clock that night in front of the Opéra Drugstore.

"How will I recognize you?"

"Forget about it. Believe me, I know you. Come on your own. No funny business, either, or she'll know about it, I guarantee you that."

Richard agreed. His caller had already hung up.

His reaction echoed Alex's just a few hours before: he reached for a bottle of scotch and took a long slug straight from it. Then Richard went to the cellar to make sure that nothing had been disturbed down there. The doors were all locked, so all was well from that angle.

Who was this guy? A criminal, obviously. But he wasn't interested in a ransom, or not for now, anyway. He wanted something else, but what could it be?

The man had said nothing about Eve. In the early days of Vincent's captivity, Richard had been at pains to conceal every trace of his presence. He had even laid off the predecessors of Lise and Roger, these two having been taken on only once the situation with Eve was somewhat "normalized." At first, he had been afraid lest the police pick up his trail. That Vincent's parents had not given up hope in the investigation he knew from the local papers. True, everything had gone smoothly: he had cornered Vincent in the middle of the night and in the middle of nowhere, and he had studiously covered his tracks. But one could never be quite sure. He had, after all, lodged a complaint concerning the attack on Viviane, and the possibility of a connection being made through some fortuitous circumstance could not be dismissed.

But then time had passed: six months, a year, soon two years—and now it was four years. The matter was surely dead and buried.

Besides, had this fellow known who Eve was, he would not have talked as he had, not have said "your wife." He thought he and Eve were married. On those occasions when Lafargue went out in public with Eve, people tended to assume that he had taken a young lover. For the last four years he had had no contact at all with his old friends, who attributed this sudden withdrawal to Viviane's collapse into insanity. Poor Richard, they thought, this second blow was too much: first his wife dies in that plane crash ten years ago, then his daughter ends up in the mental hospital.

The only people Lafargue allowed to see Eve were acquaintances or colleagues from work who saw nothing odd about his appearing now and again at a social function with a woman on his arm. The admiring murmurs elicited on these rare occasions by his "mistress" nevertheless filled Lafargue with a certain, as it were, professional pride.

So this thug could know nothing at all about Vincent. That much was obvious. But then what did he want?

Lafargue was early for the rendezvous with Alex. He paced up and down the sidewalk, jostled by the customers going in and out of the drugstore. He glanced at his watch every twenty seconds or so. At last, Alex came up to him, having first made sure that the surgeon was really on his own.

Richard appraised Alex's face: it was square and brutish.

"Did you come in your car?"

Richard pointed to the Mercedes, which was parked nearby.

"Let's go."

Alex signaled Richard to get behind the wheel and start the engine. He had taken his Colt from his pocket and placed it in his lap. Richard looked at the guy out of the corner of his eye, hoping to detect some weak spot from his demeanor. To begin with, Alex said nothing but "Straight ahead," "Turn left," and "Turn right." The Mercedes left the Opéra district behind and took a meandering route through Paris, from Place de la Concorde to the Seine embankment and then from Place de la Bastille to Place Gambetta. Alex's eyes were fastened on the rearview mirror, and he didn't engage Richard in conversation until he was absolutely certain that Lafargue had not alerted the cops.

"You're a surgeon, right?"

"Yes, I run the reconstructive surgery department at—"

"I know that. You have a clinic in Boulogne as well. Your daughter is in the crazy house in Normandy. You see, I know a lot about you. And your wife. She's not in bad shape right now—she's chained to a radiator in a cellar. You'd better listen good, or you'll never see her again. I saw you the other day on the tube."

"I gave an interview a month ago."

"You were going on about how you fix people's noses, how you can make old women's wrinkled faces all smooth again, stuff like that."

Richard understood now. He sighed. This jerk had no interest in Eve; all he was interested in was himself.

"I'm wanted by the police. I did a cop. I'm screwed, unless I get my mug changed. And you are going to change it for me. On the box, you said it didn't take long. I'm on my own: there's nobody in this thing with me. I've got nothing to lose. If you try and tell the cops, your wife is going to starve to death in that cellar. Don't try to pull anything—I tell you I've got nothing to lose. I'll take it out of her hide. If you get me busted, I'll never tell the cops where I've put her, and she'll die of hunger. Not a nice death, either."

"All right. I agree."

"Are you sure that—"

"Naturally, you must promise not to harm her."

"You love her, don't you?"

Richard's voice was toneless. He heard himself answer "yes."

"How do we do it? You take me into your hospital—no, I figure your private clinic would be the best."

Richard's hands were clamped to the steering wheel. Somehow he had to talk the guy into going to Le Vésinet. Plainly, he was no mental giant. The naïveté of his plan was proof enough of that. The idea that once under anesthesia he would be utterly at Richard's mercy had not even crossed his mind! He was an imbecile who really thought that he could pull his scheme off simply because he was holding Eve captive. It was ridiculous! All the same, he had to agree to going to Le Vésinet. At the clinic, Lafargue's hands would be tied, and the guy's stupid plan might just succeed, because Richard would never, ever go to the police.

"Listen. We'll need to save time. Any operation has to be planned way in advance. You have to be examined, as I'm sure you realize."

"Don't take me for a fool."

"No, no, but if you come to the clinic you'll be asked questions. Surgery has to be scheduled, there's a procedure that has to be followed…"

"You mean you're not the big boss?" Alex was taken aback.

"Of course I am. But, I mean, if you are wanted, you surely want to be seen by as few people as possible?"

"Yeah. So?"

"So let's go to my home. I'll show you what I can do, design a new nose for you. You also have a double chin, which we can eliminate—all that sort of thing."

Alex was suspicious, but he went along. He told himself everything was going just fine. The doctor was obviously scared shitless about his woman.

Back at Le Vésinet, Lafargue motioned Alex to a

comfortable chair. They were in his study. Richard went through one file of photographs after another until he found pictures of a man not unlike Alex in appearance. With a white marker he carefully erased the nose, then limned a new one in black. Alex watched fascinated. Lafargue moved on to the double chin. Then he rapidly produced a freehand sketch of Alex as he was now, full face and in profile, and another of the Alex that was to be.

"Great! Make me look like that and you won't have to worry about your wife."

Then Alex grabbed the first sketch and tore it up.

"You'd better not make an Identi-Kit portrait of me after the operation," he said anxiously, "and give it to the cops."

"Don't be silly. The only thing I care about is getting Eve back."

"That's her name, Eve? Anyway, don't get the idea I don't have every angle covered."

Lafargue had no illusions. This joker surely meant to kill him if ever the operation was performed. As for Eve...

"We have no time to lose, you understand. I must examine you before the operation can be done. Down in the cellar I have a small laboratory set up, so we can get started right away."

Alex frowned.

"You mean here?"

"Well, yes." Richard smiled. "I frequently work away from the hospital."

They both stood up, and Richard led the way. The cellar was very large, and there were several doors. Lafargue opened one, switched on the light, and went in. Alex followed, his eyes widening at the sight of the long, fully equipped bench and the glass-fronted cabinet stuffed with surgical instruments. Colt in hand, he went slowly round the mini-operating room that Richard had set up. He stood in front of the table, examined the immense spotlight that presided over it, picked up an anesthesiologist's mask, touched the carboys.

"What is all this?" he asked in astonishment.

"It's my laboratory, of course."

"You don't operate on people down here, do you?" Alex gestured toward the bench and spotlight. He recognized much of the equipment from the medical television show.

"No, no. But, you know, we have to perform experiments. On animals and so on."

Richard felt the sweat gathering at his brow, his heart beginning to pound, but strove to betray nothing of the fear that gripped him.

Alex nodded in bemusement. Of course, he told himself, everyone knew that doctors were always experimenting on monkeys and stuff like that.

"But then, what I think is, I won't have to go to the clinic. You could just operate on me here, couldn't you? You've got everything you need right here, don't you?"

Lafargue's hands were trembling. He thrust them into his pockets.

"Come on! You got a problem with that?"

"No, not really. I may require a few items."

"How long will I have to stay in bed after the op?"

"Oh, not long at all. You are young and strong—and we are not talking about a particularly traumatizing procedure."

"Can the bandages come off quickly?"

"Oh, no. They'll have to stay on for about a week."

Alex paced around the room, thinking it over, fingering the equipment.

"If you do it here, is it dangerous?"

Lafargue spread his arms: no, there was, as a matter of fact, no danger at all.

"You'll be all on your own? No nurse?"

"Oh, there's no need for that. I can handle everything. I just have to take my time."

Alex burst out laughing and clapped the doctor heartily on the back.

"You know what we'll do then? I'll move in here, and you'll do the job as soon as you can. What about tomorrow?"

"Yes, all right, tomorrow if you wish. But, while you are, um, convalescing, who will take care of Eve?"

"Don't get hot and bothered. She's in good hands."

"But I thought you were alone?"

"Well, no, not exactly. Don't bother about it—nobody is going to hurt her. You do the op tomorrow. We both stay here for a week. You can call your chauffeur and tell him not to come. We'll go together and get the stuff you need. You'll have to take time off from the hospital. Come on, let's go."

They went up to the ground floor. Alex got Richard to call Roger at his house. When Lafargue got off the phone, Alex pointed the way upstairs and steered him into Eve's flat.

"She's not right, your wife, is she? Why do you lock her up?"

"She…Well, she has odd attitudes."

"Like your daughter?"

"In a way, sometimes."

Alex drew the three bolts and bade Lafargue goodnight. After inspecting the other bedroom, he took a stroll round the grounds. This "Eve" must be beginning to find the time long out there in Livry-Gargan. But everything was going great. In ten days, once his bandages were off, he would kill Lafargue, and goodnight one and all. Wouldn't Eve be dead in ten days' time? But who cared?

The next morning, Alex woke Richard early. He found him lying fully clothed on the bed. Alex made breakfast, and they ate together.

"We're going to your clinic to get the things you need. Can you operate on me this afternoon?"

"No, you have to be examined, have a blood test."

"Oh, yeah. Urine test and all that."

"When I have the results, we can proceed. Tomorrow morning, all being well."

Alex was satisfied. The doc seemed straight. It was Alex who took the wheel of the Mercedes for the trip to Boulogne. He let Lafargue off outside the clinic.

"Don't be long. I've got my eye on you."

"Never fear. I'll just be a minute."

Richard went into his office. His secretary was surprised to see him so early. He asked her to let the hospital know that he would not be there for morning consultations. He delved in a drawer and chose two bottles of medicine at random. Then, after a moment's reflection, he went and got a box of scalpels, which he thought would impress Alex and strengthen his belief that he was genuinely part of the process.

Sure enough, once Lafargue was back in the car, Alex studied the labels on the bottles, opened the case containing the blades, and then put everything away carefully in the glove compartment. On arriving at Le Vésinet, they went straight down to the laboratory. Lafargue drew blood from the felon, crouched over a microscope, vaguely examined the slide using any old reagents, and then took Alex's medical history.

"Good. We won't have to wait until tomorrow. You are in excellent health. You'll rest all day. No food at lunchtime. And then, this evening, I'll operate on you."

He went over to Alex and felt his nose, then his neck. From his pocket, Alex produced the sketch of his new face and unfolded it.

"Just like this?"

"Yes, just like that."

On Lafargue's bed, with Lafargue safely locked in the wife's rooms, Alex lounged for several hours. He would have liked a drink, but that was not allowed. About six o'clock, he went to get the surgeon. He was tense: the idea of being on an operating table had always frightened him. Richard reassured him and got him to undress. Reluctantly, Alex parted with his Colt.

"Don't forget your wife, Doc," muttered Alex as he lay down.

Richard turned the large spotlight on. Its white light was dazzling. Alex blinked. After a moment, Lafargue appeared at his side in white coat and surgical mask. Alex smiled with relief.

"Are we ready?" asked Lafargue.

"Ready. And no tricks—or you'll never see your wife again."

Richard went and closed the door of the operating room, took a syringe, and came back over to Alex.

"This injection will make you relax. Then, in about fifteen minutes, I'm going to put you to sleep."

"Yeah. But no tricks!"

The tip of the needle slid delicately into a vein. Alex saw the surgeon above him, smiling.

"I said no tricks, okay?"

Suddenly, he was asleep. In his last second of consciousness, Alex sensed that something was not quite right.

Richard tore off the mask, extinguished the spotlight, and hoisted the inert Alex onto his shoulder. Opening the door to the operating room, he went out into the passage and staggered under the weight to another cellar door.

After turning the key in the lock, he carried Alex over to the moss-covered wall. The sofa and armchairs were still in place, along with various belongings of Vincent's. He chained Alex to the wall, tightening the shackles by a few links. He went back to the operating room for a needle and catheter, which he attached to a vein in Alex's forearm; he knew that once Alex woke up he would still be able, chained as he was, to wriggle enough to prevent him from administering another shot. Lafargue was quite sure that this guy, desperate and wanted by the police, would find the strength to resist "classic" forms of torture, at least for a time. And time was something Richard did not have. For now, he waited.

Tossing his scrubs on the floor, he went upstairs for a bottle of scotch and a glass. Then he came back down and settled into an armchair facing Alex. He had administered a low dose of the anesthetic, and his prisoner was bound to awake before long.

2

Alex was slow to come around. Lafargue waited, watching his reactions. He got up and slapped him hard to hasten the return of consciousness.

Alex saw his chains, the cellar cluttered with furniture, the weird trompe-l'oeil windows, sea, and mountains. He sniggered. It was all over. He wouldn't ever say where that bitch was. Not even if he was tortured. Death didn't matter to him now.

The doctor watched him from the armchair, sipping from a glass. It was whisky—the bottle was by him on the floor. The bastard! He had made a complete fool of him; he'd been laughing at him all along. But you had to say it he was quite a guy, he had never lost his cool—a real con artist. And, yes, Alex had to admit it, he himself was truly pathetic.

"So that's it, is it? Eve is in a cellar, chained to a radiator. Alone."

"She's going to croak. You'll never find out where she is." Alex was jabbering.

"Did you brutalize her?"

"No. I wanted to jump her bones, but I decided to put it off till later. I guess I should have done it, huh? Mind you, nobody will ever fuck her now. Never. Where she is, no one will show up for at least two weeks. She's bound to die of hunger and thirst. And it's your fault. Maybe one day you'll see her skeleton. Was she a good lay, at least?"

"Be quiet," said Lafargue softly, through clenched teeth. "You're going to tell me where she is."

"No way, asshole. Cut me up into little pieces if you want. I won't tell you a thing. I'm for it, I know that. If you don't kill me, the cops will get me. I've had it, and I don't give a shit."

"How wrong you are, you poor fool. You'll talk, I promise you."

Richard went over to Alex, who spat in his face. The surgeon had fastened Alex's arm to the wall, palm facing outward; the wrist was chained, and long strips of extra-strong packing tape stuck to the concrete prevented the slightest movement of the limb.

"Look here," said Richard.

He pointed to the catheter already inserted into Alex's vein. Alex began to sweat and to sob. The bastard was going to get the better of him after all. By using a drug.

Richard showed him a syringe, which he attached to the catheter. Gently, he pressed the plunger. Alex screamed, and tugged vainly on his chains.

The fluid was inside him, flowing through his veins. A wave of nausea washed over him, then his mind grew more and more fuzzy. He stopped shouting and wriggling. As his eyes glazed over, he could still see Lafargue's smiling face and mean expression.

"What's your name?"

Alex's head had subsided onto his chest, but Richard grabbed his matted hair and wrenched it upright again.

"Barny. Alex Barny."

"Do you remember my wife?"

"Yes."

A very few minutes later, Alex gave up the address of the house in Livry-Gargan.

❖

A breath of air is making its way across the floor. You twist, and turn on your side, and press your cheek to the ground so as to relish this trace of coolness. Your throat is painful, dry. The adhesive tape across your lips tugs at the skin.

The door opens. The light goes on. It is Mygale. He rushes to you. Why does he seem so stricken? He takes you in his arms, gently pulls the tape from your mouth, covers your face with kisses. He calls you "my baby" and sets to work on the cord, untying it. Your swollen limbs hurt, but your circulation is quickly restored once the restraints are gone.

Mygale holds you tight, pressing himself against you. He runs his fingers through your hair, strokes your head, the nape of your neck. He picks you up from the floor and bears you out of the room.

You are not at Le Vésinet but in some other house. What does it all mean? Mygale kicks a door open. You are in a kitchen now. Without putting you down, he takes a glass, fills it with water and has you drink it slowly, in tiny sips.

You feel as though you have swallowed kilos of dust, and nothing has ever given you such a delightful sensation as this water in your mouth.

Mygale carries you into a crudely furnished living room. He sets you down in an armchair, kneels in front of you, places his head against your belly and his arms about your waist.

You follow all this with detachment, like the spectator of some meaningless game. Mygale disappears, only to return with the bedspread, which has been left behind. He wraps you in it and carries you outside. It is night.

The Mercedes is waiting in the street. Mygale puts you in the passenger seat and gets behind the wheel.

He talks to you. He is telling a crazy, completely unbelievable tale. You hardly listen. A criminal is supposed to have kidnapped you so as to have a hold over Mygale. Poor Mygale: he has gone mad; he can no longer tell reality from his fantasy world. As for the tenderness he is showing you, you are certain that he will make you pay for it in suffering. At a stop light he turns to you, smiles, strokes your hair once more.

At Le Vésinet, he carries you into the drawing room and sits you on a sofa. He runs up to your room and fetches a robe. He helps you into it, then vanishes again. This time he reappears with a tray laden with food and drink. He hands you a few pills; you don't know what they are, and you don't care.

He gets you to eat, coaxing you into swallowing yogurt and fruit.

Once you finish eating, your eyes close all by themselves: you are all in. He carries you upstairs, lays you in your bed; before falling asleep, you notice that he has sat down next to you and taken your hand.

You wake up. There is a pale radiance: it must be early morning. Mygale is there, close to you, asleep in an armchair, and your bedroom door is wide open.

Your legs are still sore: the cord was tied very tight. You turn onto your side to see Mygale better. You think back to the preposterous story he told you in the car. Something about a gangster? Yes, a criminal on the lam who wanted Mygale to alter his face. And you were the hostage!

You are not sure about it anymore. Sleep is returning. A sleep punctuated by nightmares. Always the same images: Mygale is cackling; you are laid out on a long table beneath a blinding spotlight. Mygale wears a white surgeon's smock and hat, and he laughs wildly.

In your perception his laugh is amplified, and it hurts your ears; you wish you could sleep longer, but no, the anesthesia has worn off. You are coming back from elsewhere, the dream images are still vivid, and Mygale is laughing. You turn your head, and see that your arm—no, both arms, are restrained. A needle is sticking in the crook of one arm, attached to a tube through which liquid falls drop by drop from a flask of serum waving gently way up above your head. You feel dizzy, and then, little by little, you are assailed by violent shooting pains from farther down, from your lower belly. And Mygale laughs.

Your thighs are parted, and you are hurting. Your knees are clamped into supports of tubular steel, as though you were on one of those tables used by gynecologists to examine...God, it hurts! The pain spreads from your genitals into your abdomen; you try to lift your head, to see what is happening to you—and Mygale is still laughing.

"Hold on, little Vincent. Let me help you."

Mygale has picked up a mirror and, grasping you by the nape of the neck, he holds it between your legs. All you can see in the glass is a mass of bloody dressings, and two tubes hooked up to bottles.

"Soon, very soon, you'll see everything better." Mygale is apoplectic with laughter.

But you understand what he has done to you. First the injections, the developing breasts—and now this.

When all trace of the anesthetic's effect was gone and you were fully conscious, you screamed and screamed for a very long while. He had left you there in his operating room, flat on your back, bound to the bench.

He came back at last. Leaned over you, still laughing. Would he ever stop laughing?

He had brought a cake, a little cake with a candle on it. Just one.

"My dear Vincent, we are going to celebrate the first birthday of someone you are going to know very well: Eve."

He gestured toward your belly.

"There's nothing there anymore. I'll explain everything. But you are not Vincent anymore. You are Eve."

He cut the cake, took a slice, and mashed it into your face. You hadn't the strength even to cry out. Grinning, Mygale ate his own piece. Then he uncorked a bottle of champagne, filled two flutes, drank his, and flung the contents of the other over your head.

"So, my little Eve, have you nothing else to say for yourself?"

You asked him what he had done to you. It was very simple, he told you. He proceeded to push the examining table into the other cellar room, the room where you had been imprisoned for so long.

"My dear girl, I'm afraid I was not able to take photographs of the surgery I have just performed on you. But since it is a very common procedure, I can explain it to you by means of a short film."

He started a projector, and on a screen hung on one wall an operating room soon appeared. An off-screen voice, not Mygale's, delivered a commentary.

"Following a hormonal treatment lasting two years, we are able to perform a vaginoplasty on Monsieur X, with whom we have had numerous preparatory consultations.

"We begin, after anesthesia, by cutting away a flap of the glans penis 1.2 centimeters in length, then we detach the entirety of the skin of the shaft of the penis down to the root. Next we dissect the pedicle, likewise to the root. We proceed in an identical manner with respect to the dorsal vasculo-nervous pedicle of the penis. The aim is to bring the anterior layer of the corpora cavernosa down over the root of the penis."

You could not take your eyes off the spectacle of these men in surgical gloves with their scalpels and forceps, cutting into flesh as Mygale had cut into your flesh.

"A second intervention calls for a scroto-perineal incision 3 centimeters in front of the anus, the exteriorization of the penis through this incision, and the continued dissection of the skin and the flap of the glans penis.

"Here we continue to isolate the urethra and separate the corpora cavernosa along the median line."

Mygale laughed and laughed. He got up from time to time to adjust the focus and pat you on the cheek.

"A third stage involves the construction of a neovagina 4 centimeters wide and 12–16 centimeters in depth. Here we see the closing of the anterior extremity of the sheath of the penis and the invagination of the skin of the penis into the neovagina.

"The glans flap is exteriorized so as to form a neoclitoris. The skin of the scrotum, which has been kept very thin, is itself resected and will serve to create the labia majora.

"Here we see the same patient several months later. The outcome is very satisfactory: the vagina is a good size and completely functional; the clitoris is perfectly active and sensitive; and the urethral orifice is well positioned and attended by no urinary complications."

The film was over. You had an itching sensation amid the pain in your lower belly. You wanted to urinate. He had introduced a drain, and it was by way of the resulting strange sensation that you arrived at a new perception of your sexual parts. You cried out once more.

It was awful; you could not get to sleep. Mygale shot you up with tranquilizers. Later on, he undid your restraints to get you on your feet. Taking tiny steps, you walked round in circles. The drain dangled between your legs along with the two tubes, each leading to a vacuum bottle that was supposed to suck up your secretions. Mygale held one bottle, and the other was thrust into the pocket of your robe. You had no strength at all. Mygale soon took you out of the cellar and set you up in a small flat.

There was a dressing room, a bedroom…The light blinded you, for this was the first time you had left your prison in two years. The sunshine bathed your face deliciously.

Your "convalescence" lasted a very long time. The drain disappeared, the two bottles also. All that was left was that hole, down there between your legs. Mygale obliged you to have a plug in your vagina all the time; otherwise, he said, the skin would close up. You kept it inside you for months and months. There was a very sensitive place there, too, just above: your clitoris.

The door to your bedroom was always locked. Through the slats of the closed shutters, you could see grounds, a little pond, some swans. Mygale came to see you every day, spending long hours with you. Speaking to you about your new life. About the person—the woman—you had become.

You took up the piano again, and painting. Since you now had breasts and that hole down between your thighs, you had no choice but to go along. What good would running away do? Going back home after such a long time? Could the place Vincent had once known even be called home? What would the people who had known him say? No, you had no real choice. All the makeup, the dressing, the perfume…And then, to top it off, Mygale took you one day to the Bois de Boulogne. After that, you were beyond hope.

Today, the man is sleeping near you. He must be uncomfortable crammed into that armchair. When he found you in the cellar, he kissed you, he took you in his arms. The bedroom door is open. What does he want now?

Richard opened his eyes. His back ached. He had a strange sensation: he had spent the whole night watching over Eve, but now a rustle of fabric—the sheet, perhaps—suggested that Eve was awake, watching him in the first light of day. There she was, in the bed, her eyes wide open. Richard smiled, got to his feet, stretched, and went to sit on the edge of the bed. When he spoke, he fell back absurdly into the polite form of address, a habit that he had instituted and which he abandoned only during his hate-filled obscene tirades.

"Are you feeling better? It's all over. I mean, it's finished—you can leave. I'll take care of the paperwork, your new identity. That's the usual thing. You understand? You'll go to the police, tell them everything…"

Richard was admitting defeat and couldn't stop. He was pitiful. His defeat was total, humiliating—but it came too late to punish a hatred that was already extinct.

Eve got up, took a bath, and dressed. She went down to the drawing room. Richard found her by the pond. He had come with crumbled bread, which he threw to the swans. She crouched by the waterside and whistled to the birds. They cruised over and bowed their necks to take the morsels of bread from her hand.

The day was splendid. The two of them made for the house together and sat side by side in the swing by the swimming pool. They stayed there a good while, close together, without a word.

"Richard?" said Eve at last, "I want to see the sea."

He turned toward her, looked at her with immense sadness, and nodded. They went back inside. Eve went off to find a bag and stuff a few things in it. Richard waited for her in the car.

They set off. She lowered her window and played at resisting the wind, extending her hand outside the car. He suggested she stop, for fear that insects or flying gravel might hurt her.

Richard drove fast, devouring the curves in a kind of frenzy. She asked him to slow down. Before long, the seaside cliffs came into view.

The pebble beach of Etretat was black with people. Vacationers jammed the water's edge. It was low tide. The two walked along the beachfront and followed the foot of the cliffs through the tunnel that leads to another beach where the Hollow Needle stands.

Eve asked Richard whether he had read a novel by Maurice Leblanc, a wild tale of bandits holed up in a cavern carved out of the inside of a cliff. No, he had not read it. He laughed as he answered her, with a nuance of bitterness, as much as to say that his profession left him precious little leisure time. But Eve did not give up: how could anyone not know Arsène Lupin?

Retracing their steps, they headed back to the town. Eve was hungry. They took a table on the terrace of a seafood restaurant. She set about a plateful of oysters and whelks. Richard toyed with a spider-crab claw, then let her finish eating on her own.

"Richard, what's all this about a gangster, anyway?"

He told her all over again: his return to Le Vésinet, her empty bedroom, the bolts drawn, his alarm at her disappearance. And how he had found her.

"What about this thug? Did you let him go?" Eve was still skeptical and wary.

"No, he's chained up in the cellar."

His response was delivered in a low, expressionless voice. For a moment Eve could hardly breathe.

"Richard! You've got to go down there. You can't just leave him there to die!"

"He hurt you. That's exactly what he deserves."

She pounded her fist on the table to bring him back to

reality. The white wine in her glass, the half-eaten crab on the table, and this inappropriate talk about a guy rotting in the cellar at Le Vésinet—all conspired to give her the impression of being in some surreal play. As for Richard, he was gazing vacantly into the distance. She felt sure that if she had asked him to throw himself from the top of those cliffs, he would have complied without thinking twice about it.

It was already late when they got back to Le Vésinet and went into the house. He led the way down the stairs to the cellar. He opened the door and turned the light on. The guy was there, sure enough, on his knees, his arms stretched wide by the chains she knew so well. When Alex lifted his head, Eve gave out a long cry like the wail of a wounded animal unable to grasp what is happening to it.

Doubled over, barely breathing, she pointed a finger at the prisoner. Then she rushed out into the passage, fell to her knees, and vomited. Richard, who had followed her out, supported her and pressed his hand to her brow.

So this was it. This was the last act. Mygale had dreamed up this whole gangster story, this entire grotesque tale, simply to calm your suspicions. He had tamed you with tenderness, giving in to your whimsical desire to see the sea, only to plunge you back into endless horror!

And this trick of having you discover Alex as a prisoner, just like you four years ago, had the sole purpose of breaking you even further, of driving you even closer (as if that were possible) to the brink of madness.

Yes, that was his plan. Not to humiliate you by forcing you into prostitution, after first castrating you, hacking you up, mutilating you—after destroying your body and fabricating another one, turning you into a toy of flesh and blood. All that was just playing about, just the lead-up to his real goal, which was to drive you mad, as mad as his daughter. Since you had survived every ordeal, he had had to raise the stakes.

Step by step he had brought you low, plunging your head into the darkest waters, then yanking it up by the hair just before you drowned. And now came the coup de grace: Alex!

Mygale was not mad: he was a genius. Who else could have designed such a subtle escalation? The bastard! He had to be killed!

As for Alex, Mygale would have little use for him, as he must know. He surely had no intention of subjecting him to the same torments as you. Alex was a big oaf, a brute; he had amused you at one time: you could do whatever you wanted with him; he would have followed you anywhere, like a dog.

Mygale could do nothing with Alex: the refinements of suffering you had experienced would not be his. Perhaps Mygale intended to make you...Yes, that was it! You only had to look at Alex in his chains, naked as a worm, to see what Mygale had in mind.

One victim was not enough for him: he needed both of them at his mercy. Four years! It had taken Mygale four years to catch up with Alex. What had become of Alex in the meantime? But, above all, how had Mygale managed to find him? You knew you had never breathed a word.

Mygale was there next to you. He was holding you up. The pool of vomit was spreading on the concrete floor. Mygale murmured soft words, my love, my sweet, and fussed over you, wiping your mouth with a handkerchief.

The door to the operating room was open. You made a dash toward the table and grabbed a scalpel. Then you walked slowly toward Mygale with the blade pointed right at him.

3

They faced each other there in the crude fluorescent light of the concrete cellar. She advanced calmly, scalpel in hand. Richard stood motionless. In the next room, Alex began to shout. He had seen Eve fall to her knees, then drag herself out of his field of vision; now he could see her again, through the half-open door, as she moved forward with the blade.

"My gun, sweetheart! Come over here! He left the gun there!"

Eve came back in and picked up Alex's revolver, which was indeed still lying on the sofa. Richard had not even flinched and still stood rigid in the passage, holding his ground despite the Colt now trained on his midriff. And then he uttered a few incomprehensible words.

"Eve, I beg you, tell me what all this means!"

She stopped dead, staring at him. Was his mystification faked—another of his tricks? Well, the bastard wouldn't get away with it that easily!

"Don't worry, Alex," she shouted. "We're going to fix this shitbag once and for all!"

It was Alex's turn to be mystified. How did she know his name? Lafargue had perhaps told her? Of course, it was that simple. Lafargue had been keeping his wife locked up, and she was seizing this chance to get rid of her husband!

"Eve, kill me if you want. But at least tell me what is going on."

Richard had let himself slip down the wall to the ground, where he now sat.

"You're shitting me! You're shitting me! You're shitting me!" She had begun by murmuring the words, now she was screaming them. The muscles of her neck bulged, her eyes seemed about to spring from their sockets, and she was trembling violently.

"Eve, please, please, explain."

"Alex! Alex Barny! It's him. He was with me. He raped Viviane, too. He even fucked her in the ass, and I—and I held her down. You always thought I was on my own. I never told you different. I didn't want you going looking for him, too. It's as much his fault as mine if your daughter is insane, you bastard. But it was I who took all the punishment."

Alex was listening to the woman. What was she saying? It's the two of them, he thought; they are playing a weird game with me: trying to make me crazy. But then, as he looked closely at Lafargue's wife, there was something about the mouth, the eyes...

"Aha! You didn't know there were two of us, did you? But there were: Alex was my pal. Poor guy, he didn't get laid much. When it came to the girls, I had to, well, sort of scare them up for him. With your girl it was harder than usual. She was strictly not interested! Feeling her up a bit, kissing her—she quite liked all that. But the second I got my hand up her skirt, that was it. So we had to force her a little."

Richard shook his head in disbelief, beaten down by Eve's shouting, her shrill voice still at screaming pitch.

"I went first. Alex held her. She put up a struggle. You

were in the inn, stuffing your face and dancing, weren't you? After, I let Alex take over from me. He had a lot of fun, I can tell you that, Richard. She was whimpering. She was hurt. Not as much as me, with everything you've done. I'm going to kill you, Mygale, d'you hear me?"

The truth was, Mygale had never known about Alex. You never told him. When he first told you why he had mutilated you—on account of the rape of Viviane and her going mad—you had decided to say nothing. Your only revenge was to keep Alex out of it. Mygale didn't know there had been two of you.

You were lying there on the operating table when Mygale first spoke to you about that July evening two years earlier. A Saturday. You were hanging out in the village with Alex with strictly nothing to do. The school vacation had only just begun. You were supposed to go to England soon, while Alex stayed on his father's farm working in the fields.

The two of you had visited every café and played on every table-soccer and pinball machine before both climbing onto your motorcycle. It was mild out. At Dinancourt, a fairly large town some thirty kilometers away, there was a dance and a traveling fair. Alex shot at balloons with an air rifle. As for you, you watched the girls. There were a lot of them. It was late afternoon when you first saw the kid. She was pretty. She was walking around on the arm of an old guy—or at any rate much older than her. It had to be her father. She wore a light blue summer dress. Her hair was curly and blond, and her still childlike face bore no makeup. They were part of a group, and you could easily tell from their attire that they were not country people.

The party sat down at a café terrace, but the girl continued visiting the fair on her own. You approached her, respectful as always. Her name was Viviane. And, yes, the guy with the white hair was indeed her father.

In the evening there was a dance in the village square. You asked Viviane to meet you. She would like to, but her father... They had come here for a wedding and were staying at the inn. The inn was part of an old château, some way away from the rest of the village, and functions and parties were often held there and in the grounds of the place. Viviane was supposed to go to the wedding dinner. You talked her round: all right, she would meet you here, by the frites stand. She was just a kid, a bit dopey, but very cute. As the evening wore on, you wandered over toward the château several times. The rich people had laid on a band: not a bunch of hicks with an accordion, of course, but a real band, guys in white tuxedos playing jazz. The windows of the inn had been closed to make sure the whining strains of the dance band could not waft in.

Viviane came out about ten o'clock. You bought her a drink. She had a Coke, you a scotch. You danced. Alex looked on. You winked at him. During a slow one, you kissed Viviane. You felt her heart pound in her chest. She didn't know how to kiss: she kept her lips tightly shut. When you showed her how, she started pushing as hard as she could with her tongue! She was a dimwit. She smelled good: a sweetish perfume but discreet—not like the eau de cologne the local girls sloshed all over themselves. Her dress had a plunging neckline, and as you danced you stroked her bare back.

You strolled through the village, and you kissed her again. A bit better this time: she had learned something. You slipped your hand under her dress and ran it up her thigh as far as her panties. She was excited, but pulled away. She said she was afraid of being chewed out by her father if she stayed out too late. You didn't insist, and you both went back to the village square. The father had left the inn in search of his daughter. He ran into the two of you, but you avoided his gaze and walked on.

You watched their exchange from a distance. At first he

seemed angry, but then he laughed and went back to the inn. Viviane came back toward you. Her father had granted her an extension.

You danced. She pressed up against you. In the half-light you fondled her breasts. An hour later she said she wanted to go back. You signaled to Alex, who was leaning against the bar near the dancing area with a can of beer in his hand. You told Viviane that you would walk her to the inn. Hand in hand, you circled the château. Laughing, you pulled her into the bushes at the edge of the place's grounds; laughing, she protested. She really wanted to stay with you.

You leaned against a tree. She was kissing just fine now. She let you pull her dress up, a little. Without warning, you grabbed her panties and ripped at them, clamping your other hand over her mouth so she could not cry out. Alex was close by. He grabbed her hands, stuffing her arms beneath her body as he forced her onto her back. He held her firmly while you knelt between her legs. Alex watched what you did.

Then it was your turn to hold Viviane in place, on all fours, as Alex positioned himself behind her. For Alex it was not enough to do to her what you had done: he wanted more. In entering her he hurt her too much; she began to struggle with strength of desperation and succeeded in breaking free. She was screaming. You went after her, grabbing her by the foot. You managed to immobilize her. You tried to slap her, but your hand balled up as you delivered the blow, and she got your fist full in the face. The back of her neck slammed into the tree trunk. She passed out, but her body continued to thrash about.

As Mygale told you afterward, when he heard Viviane's screams the band was playing "The Man I Love." He ran out into the grounds of the château. He saw you, on your knees in the grass, clutching at Viviane's ankle in your attempt to catch her and stop her screaming.

As for Alex, he had taken off without hesitation and vanished into the shrubbery. Viviane was still thrashing wildly. You had to get out of there fast. You raced straight ahead. The guy was hard on your heels. But he had just eaten a heavy meal, and you had no trouble losing him. Alex was waiting for you with the bike at the other end of the village.

For the next few days you were very nervous. The guy had seen you, first near the frites stand and then in the field behind the inn, in the split second it took you to decide which way to run. But you were not from the village, which was a good way away from your home, and little by little your fears evaporated. You left for England the next week and returned only in late August. And, after all, it wasn't the first time you had run into trouble with Alex.

Mygale had searched for a long time. He knew your approximate age. He had a rough idea of your face. He never told the police: he wanted you for himself. He combed the whole region in widening circles, covering every village. He spent hours at factory gates and outside high schools, watching.

Three months later, he spotted you in a café opposite the high school in Meaux. He followed you, spied on you, studied your habits. Until that late September evening when he fell upon you in the forest.

He knew nothing of Alex's existence; he couldn't have. That is why he is here in front of you now, exhausted, at your mercy…

Richard was stunned. Kneeling, Eve held the Colt with both hands and aimed it at him. Her arms were straight, and her index finger whitened as she pressed on the trigger.

"I am going to kill you." She chanted the words in a monotone.

"Eve, I didn't know! It's not fair!"

Nonplussed by this incongruous remorse, she let her guard down for a moment. Richard was watching, and he saw it. His foot crashed into the young woman's outstretched forearms. She dropped the weapon and cried in pain. He leaped up, snatched the Colt, and charged into the room where Alex was chained up. He fired twice. Alex collapsed, hit in the neck and in the heart.

Richard went back to the passage, leaned over and helped Eve back to her kneeling position, then he knelt down himself and held the Colt out to her.

Eve struggled to her feet, took a deep breath, set her feet wide apart and carefully brought the tip of the Colt's barrel to Lafargue's temple.

He stared at her, and his gaze betrayed no feeling at all. It was as though he wanted to project an indifference that would allow Eve to put aside all pity; as though he wanted, with his cold and impenetrable eyes, to be Mygale once more.

Eve saw Richard reduced, destroyed. She dropped the Colt.

She went up to the ground floor and ran out into the grounds, pulling up short, out of breath, at the front gate. It was a fine day, and reflected light danced on the blue water of the swimming pool.

Eve retraced her steps, went into the house, climbed the stairs. In her room, she sat down on the bed. The easel was there, covered with a piece of cloth. She tore it aside, and for a long time contemplated the vile portrait of Richard as a transvestite, the wine-ravaged face, the wrinkled skin: Richard as a ruined whore.

Very slowly, she walked back down to the cellar. Alex's

body still hung from the chains. A large pool of blood had formed on the concrete. She raised Alex's head, and for a moment held the gaze of his dead eyes. Then she left the prison.

Richard still sat in the passage, his arms dangling by his sides, his legs rigid. A slight tic animated his upper lip. She sat next to him and took his hand. She let her head fall onto his shoulder.

Her voice was barely audible.

"Come on. We can't leave the body here like this."